Requiem for a Party Girl

Sylvia Nickels

Requiem For a Party Girl
2nd Edition
Sylvia Nickels Copyright ©2018

Requiem for a Party Girl/Sylvia Nickels
ISBN-13: 978-0-9799222-5-1
ISBN-10: 0-9799222-5-9
A Different Drummer Publishing USA

1. Women private investigators - Fiction. 2. Mystery – Fiction. 3. Tennessee private investigator – Fiction. 4. Murder – Fiction.

Requiem for a Party Girl, written by Sylvia Nickels, previously published 2015 by Oconee Spirit Press, Waverly, TN

DEDICATION

To everyone who has encouraged me through all these years to keep pursuing my dream of publication, my heartfelt thanks. I have been fortunate to have the steadfast support of my immediate and extended family as well as the many talented writers in my writing groups. When my determination has flagged, family, friends and fellow writers never failed to pull me back on track to fire up the creative process once again. Their critiques and suggestions have been on point. If my books have any merit, it is most likely because of that support and those suggestions.

One

On the tv screen a perfectly coiffed female was saying "...no one has been identified and charged in the case of a prominent local resident's ordeal in the Park on Clare Creek Mountain two nights ago."

One of my favorite place names had pinged off my dozing gray cells and I jerked fully awake.

The anchor now recapped the facts as pictures of an older woman flashed on the screen. I banged the foot rest down and sat straight up in my chair. Strands of auburn hair partly covered her face and her clothing was a mess. Disheveled as she was I knew her.

I'd met her nearly three years earlier. We'd both been clients at a battered women's shelter. At the time her hair partly covered the bruise on her neck and the skin around one eye as well. The whole right side of her face was dark purple, shading into green and yellow and she winced when she turned her head too quickly.

Make-up hardly disguised the black bruise on my own face just below my dishwater blonde hairline. I'd set a cup of coffee in front of my ex and a little slopped out on the table, one of many things that infuriated him. He leapt to his feet, fist at the ready. I jumped back, but not fast enough to evade the blow. It didn't land where he'd aimed, the side of my head where my hair would cover the bruise. That hadn't been the first time, but it definitely was the last. For me, anyway. He left me lying on the floor and went out.

I lay there a few minutes, trying to stop my tears, in case he came back. He hated crying, too. Then a thread of anger rose from somewhere and I knew I had to end this abuse or one day I'd be dead by my husband's hand. A month before my friend Tabi had scribbled the number for the local women's shelter on a scrap of paper and slipped it into my hand at work. I found it and picked up the phone.

Before the unexpected jolt of memory brought on by the news clip I'd been relaxing in my second-hand though serviceable recliner, drowsily channel surfing. My thoughtless thumbing of the television remote brought up a local station and the name *Clare Creek Mountain* had resonated.

I tuned back in as the news anchor said the woman was Rhoda Jarvis, wife of State Senator Wiley Jarvis from my district. I'd never known her name at the shelter. Clients didn't share real ones. Apparently the Senator's wife had been discovered two mornings ago chained to a tree in the park. Could her husband have put her there and left her? I could well believe it after seeing how she'd looked. I'd despised the Senator even then.

I hated him even more when news reports a year ago revealed his betrayal of his duty to his local constituents. I certainly considered it betrayal. He'd persuaded the Wexler Bend City Council to turn over control and management of the Park on Clare Creek Mountain to the Tennessee State Government.

Then he'd promptly cut some kind of deal with the State Parks Commissioner to allow some areas of the park to be developed with expensive vacation homes. In my opinion, such desecration of Clare Creek Park ranked right up there with spray painting graffiti on a church.

I switched off the television set, but before I could digest the news about Mrs. Jarvis my doorbell sounded for the second time on what had been a slow Saturday.

Earlier I'd closed my office, a miniscule alcove dining area I'd repurposed, and put together my favorite peanut butter and banana sandwich. My teeth were milliseconds from the first scrumptious bite when my doorbell rang. And kept ringing. If not a client, whoever sat on my doorbell was going to regret interrupting my gastronomic indulgence.

But when I slid back the deadbolt and jerked open the door there was no unwary target for my irritation in front of me. "What the –"

I scanned from right to left through the full-view glass storm door. Whoever had rung the bell and run away was history. From the corner of my eye I caught a glimpse of yellow against the dark burgundy paint of the porch. Another yellow rose. Damn.

I retrieved the unwanted and wilted beyond redemption tribute and marched to my kitchen. I tromped on the foot-lever to raise the lid of my ancient garbage can and let it join its day-old twin, another once-yellow rose, partly covered by the banana peel from my dinner sandwich. Some unknown person had left it on my condo porch yesterday. The first was more brown than yellow now, but both roses looked pathetic lying amid my kitchen trash.

I love yellow roses. Maybe because thirty years ago when I was five my hair was the exact luminous yellow shade of the blooms on one of Grandma's prize rose bushes. By my sixteenth birthday it had darkened to its present shade. Dark red roses I can tolerate, barely. In point of fact, though, no one ever before sent me a rose of any hue. My five foot eight frame, was still passably trim, I supposed. But a security guard turned private investigator seldom encounters people who send flowers. Only one dweller in my tiny circle of friends, by a stretch, might do so. But it would be a real stretch.

The demise of Detective Sergeant Shackleford Lane's marriage had soured him on women in any role except as colleague or an occasional sortie at a sleazy motel. The second female role I knew of only from sly innuendos from his police department friends. Since I'd never been invited to a sortie with him at any kind of motel. Which I probably would not accept anyway. I liked Shac well enough as a friend. When any other feelings tried to push into our relationship I pretended not to notice.

Two

This time when I peered through the peephole I saw an actual person standing on my porch. I opened the door and blinked at Shac. "It's you."

"Well, are you going to invite me in or not?"

I stepped back and swung the door wider. "Why aren't you out chasing the usual Saturday night mayhem makers?"

"Thought I'd drop by. Had a call a few blocks away that wasn't anything." He pulled out the pack of gum he always carried in a jacket pocket. I shook my head when he held it toward me. He extracted a stick, unwrapped and stuffed it in his mouth.

"Come in then, and take a break."

"Sure." His gaze swept along the counter as he slid onto one of the two rickety wicker barstools. He half-turned and looked at my two-chair dining table that I kept pushed back against the wall, forming a kind of divider for my office.

"Are you the dust detective today?" I asked, only half joking, as I punched the on button for my Bunn coffeemaker.

"Huh? Oh, sorry. Your place looks a hell of a lot better than mine."

He raised the hand holding the crumpled silver gum wrapper to his mouth, removed the gum he'd barely chewed and stood again.

I reached for the paper but he held onto it. "I can throw out my own trash."

He knew where the trash can was so I let him. Only he didn't just throw the wrapper away. He stepped on the lever and raised the lid, reached in and picked up the yellow rose as though he'd known it would be there. I stared as he examined the bedraggled horticultural specimen from the end of its slimy, and still thorny, stem to the dull yellow petals edged with brown.

He pulled a long narrow paper evidence bag from his jacket pocket and deposited the rose in it, then began digging in my trash again. Several ancient tabloid newspapers I'd picked up on a whim at an antique-cum-junk store were stacked on the floor, waiting to be hauled to the recycle bin. I grabbed a couple of the papers and laid them on the floor beside the can for him to put the garbage on.

A four color layout on the top page showed then newly-married State Senator Jarvis, arm around a blonde beauty at least fifteen years his junior. I started to grab it back, but Shac had already dumped my discarded coffee filter and coffee grounds from the past two mornings on the picture.

"There must be some good reason for you to inspect my trash, Shac. But I'm completely baffled as to what it might be."

"This was the second one, wasn't it?" He barked, waving the wilted blossom in my direction.

"So I'm a sorry housekeeper. Are you going to arrest me?"

"It is, isn't it, Cam? Damn it, tell me."

Something in his tone made me bite back my next smart ass question.

"Yes. The first one'd be underneath it."

He lifted out the banana peel, then crusts and heels of bread without even giving me his usual chiding look for my thriftlessness. He finally reached the first yellow rose, barely recognizable as such. He put it in another paper evidence bag.

When he finished I decided I'd been patient long enough. "Now are you going to tell me why in God's name you've dug through my trash and confiscated my poor dead roses?"

"It's my job."

"Your job?"

"Damn straight."

"To dig through my garbage?"

"Who've you pissed off enough to want to kill you?"

My jaw dropped. "If I had, what would a flower have to do with it?"

"Two dead flowers. Because the last two murder victims I've seen each received a single yellow rose on two consecutive days just before their murders."

He locked eyes with me for a moment. It almost looked like fear I saw in those dark green depths. Fear for me? Then he looked down and began replacing the garbage.

"Leave that. I'll clean it up later. Get over here and tell me why you think my roses might be connected to those murders."

He ignored me and picked up the trash by the wadded up and now coffee-soaked papers. They somehow held together until he dropped them into the can and closed the lid. He laid the two evidence bags on the counter, pulled out a pen and wrote something on them. I knew the something was the date, time and place where he'd found them.

Curiosity was killing me, but the coffeemaker had stopped dripping and gurgling. So I filled two mugs and put them on the counter. When he stopped writing I said, "Well?"

"The first victim was found a week ago. Her neighbor told us about the roses. The second victim was found two nights ago. Guy she lived with knew about the roses. Second one had just been delivered that day."

I could see where he was going with this. "You stopped by yesterday afternoon to drop off that box of ammo you picked up for me."

"And a yellow rose was here on the counter. You said it'd been left on your porch earlier. By an 'anonymous admirer.'" His hands sketched quote marks in the air.

My mind jumped ahead. Two roses. After the second one the other recipients wound up dead. Murdered. A chill skittered up my spine. I had the urge to go to my bedroom, get my Glock and check to make sure it was loaded. For crying out loud, in my own kitchen with an armed police detective sitting across the counter from me.

Atlanta, GA, One Year Ago

Gloria stared at the picture of her mother, a slender woman, each shapely arm holding a blanket-wrapped infant close to her body. The beautiful young blonde's head was tilted toward the babies, but her eyes peeked upward at the camera, as though showing them off. Tears streamed down Gloria's cheeks.

If you were so proud of us, Mom, why did you give us up? Would you still be alive if you hadn't? And where is my brother?

If only Grandma Elena was still here to talk to about the hauntingly lovely young woman. Maybe if she'd known her cousin had given Gloria the picture Grandma would have opened up about her mother finally. But two days after Juanita gave it to her, Grandma had the heart attack and died. Only when, with a heavy spirit, she went through Grandma's personal things did she find the papers. In a small box, wrapped in purple tissue paper, Gloria found her mother's death certificate, her own birth certificate and adoption papers, a yellowed newspaper clipping, two letters and another picture.

The birth certificate was the shocker. Gloria had learned that she was a twin. Had her adopted mother, Teresa, known? Or Grandma? Surely Aunt Luisa had known. Had she kept that fact secret?

Gloria skimmed the news clipping, which told of the shooting of ten people at a downtown hotel, the Grand Majestic. The victims were attendees and hotel staff at a big party in one of the suites. The victims listed by name were several city officials, three young women, a maid and two servers. Why had Grandma kept a sad reminder of the murder of her daughter?

The second letter was short and addressed to Grandma. Luisa apologized that she didn't make it to Teresa's funeral. She had been away on a job. Then she said that she supposed Grandma would be raising Teresa's adopted daughter. And Grandma didn't need to worry about Gloria's birth mother ever coming around. She had passed away. On the back of the sheet, in Grandma's hand, were a few cryptic words. 'L with friend at hotel party? Hurt? Pray to Saint---', the last word trailed off. Had the sisters even known the other was in the hotel? There was no way to know because no one in the family had ever heard from Luisa again.

Three

Shac laid two photos on the counter in front of me. "Do you recognize either of these women?"

In one of the pictures a small blonde woman, who looked to be about twenty-five or so, lay on a bed, blood soaking the sheets and the frilly blue teddy she wore. I picked it up. "Causes of death?"

"Both had blunt force trauma." He gestured to the picture I held. "Her with a small heavy statue of an angel."

"Obviously not her guardian angel." I tried for flip, but I shivered again. I picked up the other photo.

The other picture showed another blonde, dressed in jeans and striped shirt, figure a little fuller than the first girl and about my height, five feet eight. One foot was encased in a Western boot, the other bare. She lay on the ground, one arm underneath her, the other outstretched, rocks scattered around her. She, too, was covered in blood.

"Used a rock on this one?"

"Not confirmed yet. But probably, before heaving her over the fence on Clare Creek Reservoir Dam."

I jerked my head up and looked at him, his jaw was clamped so tight I could trace the muscles and ligaments. "Over the dam? These are the rocks at the base of the dam?"

"Fifty, sixty feet. Never had a chance. Of course, the Medical Examiner says the first blow probably killed her anyway."

"Signs of sexual assault?"

"Neither girl."

"Who are they?"

"Ordinary women with jobs. No records."

I got the coffee pot and refilled our cups. "What do you know about them?"

"Not a lot yet. Both led regular quiet lives. First was a hostess in the restaurant at the Clare View Hotel Conference Center. The other bartender in the lounge, Gloria Tejoso. No enemies that anybody knew about." Shac's lips compressed again to a thin line. "No signs of struggle either. Maybe they knew their assailant. The first girl always took the morning shift at the restaurant. Second slept days, worked nights."

"No sexual assault. Weapons of opportunity. Different types of jobs, though at the same place. So what's the motive for killing them?"

Both single, like me. Both younger, though the second looked closer to my age. Something tickled my mind. Did that face, bruised and covered with blood, look vaguely familiar? I must have shaken my head.

"What? Have you seen her?" Shac demanded.

The fragment of memory, if that's what it was, was gone. "No. Not that I can remember. Hard to tell though."

What connection could there be between these young women and me, if I was indeed being targeted? Why? My back muscles contracted, imagining the unexpected fear overwhelming them as somebody they knew turned on them, savage blows falling on tender places. I'd experienced it. Twice, the second was the longest. A fast learner I'm not.

"Any leads at all?"

We tried for half an hour to come up with an idea besides their workplace that might connect the two murder victims.

Shac walked over to my sofa, sat down and bounced a little on it. "Got a spare blanket?"

"What?" I dropped the mugs in the sink and turned to look at him.

"Okay, I can make do with my jacket and that throw over there."

"You're planning to spend the night on my sofa?"

"Damn straight."

I shoved down the secret feeling of relief I felt. No one, not even Shac Lane, was going to get the chance to view me again as a shrinking violet to abuse or protect. I stalked to the hall closet and pulled down my favorite quilt. It had cost more than I could afford, but I'd bought it at a fall festival because it reminded me of my mother.

"You'd better not snore louder than me." I threw the quilt at him.

He caught it and mimed shock, hand over perfect white teeth. "You? Snore? I'll go get my toothbrush. Always keep a spare in the car." He slammed the door, as usual, when he went out.

I took advantage of his absence to check that no intimate feminine garments were displayed in my bathroom. Then got the extra pillow from my bed and put it on the sofa. Shac hadn't rung the doorbell to come back in, as I knew he'd have to, the door locked automatically. I walked over and looked through the peephole.

Somebody was walking fast toward my porch and it wasn't Shac. I reached out and hit the alarm button on the keypad beside the door, eye still at the peephole. Oscillating alarms sounded inside and out and a computer-generated voice blared, "Intruder alert! Intruder alert!" The person on my walk leapt to the side and disappeared from my view. My phone rang and I grabbed it.

Four

A male voice. "Storm Security. We have an alarm. Are you all right?"

"Yes. No." I slapped off the alarm. "Call the police. I'm afraid an officer is down outside my home."

"Calling. One moment." Seconds went by. "Police are on the way. Stay on the phone, please. You're safe inside?"

"Yes," I told him the officer had gone outside, not returned, and then I saw a stranger coming up my walk. Sirens sounded and in moments two police cruisers were in front of my condo. I told the security monitor the police had arrived, thanked him and hung up the phone.

I jerked the door open as a young cop I knew, Don Mears, rang the bell.

"Did you see Shac? Is he okay?"

"He was hit on the head, my partner's with him, ambulance is on the way. What happened, Cam?"

"How bad is it? Is he conscious?" I tried to get past him, but he blocked me and gently pushed me back inside.

I pulled loose and stepped back, crossing my arms. In spite of my best efforts, I felt tears sting the back of my eyes. I forced them back and swallowed the baseball in my throat. Shac had to be okay.

"What happened, Cam? Chief Tawson will be here any minute. He'll wanta know."

"He thought I might be the next victim. Of the yellow rose killer. He was going to stay the night on my sofa. Went out to get his toothbrush. But he didn't come back."

"He thought -? Never mind. So you went out?"

"I looked through the peephole. Somebody, not Shac, was coming up my walk and I hit the alarm."

"Who was it?"

Just then the doorbell rang again and Don opened the door. Wexler Bend's Chief of Detectives DeWitt Tawson filled the opening. Black eyes in his dark brown face bored into me. He gave a faint nod toward the door and Don slipped out.

Tawson's size and bearing usually intimidated me, echoing memories I didn't want to revisit, but my anxiety for Shac overrode it. "Tell me about Shac. He's not..."

He ignored my question. "Why was Detective Lane here, Ms. Locke?"

I clenched my fists and bit back the answer I wanted to give. 'None of your damn business.' This was Shac's boss. "Detective Lane knew that someone had left me two yellow roses. He thought there might be a connection with the two murders he's investigating."

"Two yellow roses. When?" He demanded.

"The second one came today. Tell me about Shac. Please."

I must have sounded desperate. Maybe the few streaks of silver in his full head of hair meant he'd managed to retain some compassion in spite of his job. Or maybe it was the second yellow rose. He relented. "He's conscious, EMS says probably be all right. Hard head and a glancing blow. But the hospital will likely keep him overnight. Sit down and tell me what happened here. And start at the beginning."

So I did.

When I finished he asked, "Has Emory Locke contacted you recently?"

I blinked. Why was he asking about my ex-husband? "Of course not. He'd be violating a restraining order." I added, "And as far as I know, he's in Miami."

He looked at me and made no reply. We both knew restraining orders were hardly worth the paper they were printed on as far as keeping men from the women they wanted to pound.

He opened his cell phone and made a call to a colleague in Florida. While he waited for an answer to his query I went to the counter separating kitchen and living room, leaned against it. I sighed, trying for frightened female without overdoing it, Tawson was no fool. I reached behind me and flipped the two victim photos face down.

"Thanks for checking." Tawson clicked off his phone and told me that my non-beloved ex was apparently no longer in the Sunshine state. "Was the person you saw Emory Locke?"

"I don't know. It was too dark to tell."

"The street light nearest your door is out. And the bulb in your porch light is loose. Do you know how long it's been that way?"

"No. I haven't had occasion to turn it on the last couple of days."

"I assume Locke knows you still live here."

"Emory is a sorry specimen, but he's not a multiple killer."

"Willing to bet your life on it?" He challenged. "We'll take you to a safe house."

"No, I have an alarm system, I'm legally armed. I won't be chased from my own home."

"I'll order extra patrols through the area, but we don't have a man to station here full-time." He stood and straightened his jacket.

"I'd like to see Shac. I feel responsible that he's hurt."

He didn't dispute me, and I did feel responsible, God knows why. Shac was on the job when he came to question me, and I hadn't asked him to stay. But he'd gone to his car for his toothbrush because he'd intended to protect me even if I hadn't asked. I owed him.

"Not tonight. He needs rest."

Tawson left and I reset the alarm. I got my Glock from a drawer of the bedside table and made sure the clip was fully loaded with a shell chambered. After checking all the windows and my back door, I went to the counter and picked up the pictures Shac had brought. If he ever found out I'd had them when he talked to me, Captain Tawson would be way beyond a happy camper that I hadn't handed them over to him. But I wanted to study them. Maybe I'd see something that would trigger the elusive memory again.

After half an hour of examining the photos of the two unfortunate women with my magnifying glass I was no closer to an answer. Why them? Why yellow roses? If I had indeed been targeted as the killer's third victim, he had been denied his goal tonight. Would he try again? I didn't believe he would. But then I've been wrong before. And had the scars to prove it.

I made myself turn out the lights and lie on my bed. But I couldn't make myself change into my ratty polka dot flannel pajamas. After staring at the ceiling for what seemed like hours, Glock beside me, I must have fallen into a light doze.

Five

The next thing I knew I was on my feet, yanked awake by three separate and what seemed like simultaneous sounds - shattering glass, a shrieking alarm and the mechanical voice warning of an intruder.

I backed into a corner, grasping my Glock with both hands in front of me. I strained to hear something, anything, before the security call added the telephone bell to the din. Just then, I realized I felt a draft of cool air sweep through the room. I kept my eyes glued to the faintly outlined doorway as I picked up the receiver on the bedside table.

"Ms. Locke? The police are on the way again. Are you okay?"

"Yes. But I think somebody broke a window. I feel a draft and the sirens sound loud." The irrelevant thought crossed my mind that my neighbors would probably start a petition for the Condo Association to force me out any day now.

The sirens stopped in front and somebody pounded on my door. Why didn't they ring the doorbell? When I tried to turn on the living room light, I figured out why. I opened the door and saw Don Mears outlined in the light of the now functional street light. But the porch light was not, although I'd left it turned on when I went to bed. I glanced at the switch beside the door amd saw that it was still in the 'on' position.

He had to raise his voice to be heard over the alarm. "Cam? Are you all right? Why's this light off?"

"I left it on." I slapped the alarm off as I spoke and my voice sounded too loud. "Breaking glass and the alarm woke me up."

Don shined his flashlight around. I grabbed the one I kept under the counter with my left hand, gun still in my right.

The light from my flash wobbled a little. I was trained in using a weapon, but I still wouldn't have been surprised if Don had asked me to put it down. We both swung our flashlight beams toward the window in the side wall of my living room. He pulled the curtain aside. The window was intact. He motioned for me to stay behind him and started down the hall.

He stopped at the first door, which was actually the master bedroom, now my guest/storeroom. I slept in the smaller bedroom since kicking Emory out. I also got rid of all of the furniture and the belongings he'd left-behind. The uncurtained and unfurnished room held only the few boxes and odds and ends I'd tossed there, the window also intact.

As we entered my bedroom I felt liquid running down my forehead and into my right eye. I lifted the hand holding my flashlight and brushed it away with my wrist. The light from our flashlights hit my bed and sparks of light shot back from broken glass scattered on the bedspread. A large rock lay near the foot of the bed. Don spoke into his shoulder mike as his flashlight jerked up to the window above the bed. "Lars, check for footprints under the back window."

Don turned slowly in a circle, gun following his flashlight. When the light reached me, it stabbed into my eyes. He lowered his weapon and swore softly. He grabbed my arm and sat me down on the bench at the foot of my bed. "You're hurt, there's blood on your face."

I looked at my hand, red was smeared from wrist to knuckles. Up to then I hadn't felt a thing, but now I realized the right side of my head was a mass of pain.

Two other cops came in. Don's partner, Lars something, his last name skittered away through the pain, nodded toward me. His eyes widened slightly as they moved to a spot on my head. He said something to Don. Through a slight buzz in my ears I heard Don talking to Dispatch.

"We need an ambulance again. Rock through Locke's bedroon window hit her head. Gashed it." He paused. "Okay, I think. Better get it checked out." He waited a minute. "Yeah, electric meter to her condo pulled loose in the building utility room." Another pause. "Dangerous as hell.

Coulda electrocuted himself. Call the power company, get the juice cut off."

He came over and knelt in front of me. "Heads up, Cam. Ambulance will be here in a second. You heard?"

I nodded. Big mistake. The room swam.

Don looked around. The emergency light I kept charged in a hallway outlet gave some illumination but not much. "So how is it the alarm still functioned? Isn't it electric?"

"Battery backup. Connected to a golf cart battery in the front closet. I'm not about to depend on a couple of nine volts."

He smiled, patted my hand. "Good thing."

More sirens. The ambulance. I started to get up, but Don put a gentle hand on my shoulder as two hefty paramedics rolled a gurney down my hallway.

"Stay put. You get wheels."

Surrendering to his orders I grabbed my blue-denim tote bag from the floor and climbed on the gurney. In the ambulance they dabbed at the gash on my head, pronounced it not too bad and they'd let the ER doc dress it. All the way to the hospital they debated the relative merits of various painkillers and when they should be given. I offered ten hours of free private detective services for even the least effective one and they laughed.

When we arrived at the ER the heartless, well, probably not really heartless, EMTs wheeled me in and turned me over to the triage nurse. She clucked over my head wound, made notes on a chart and asked about next-of-kin.

Slightly unnerved, I told her there was no next-of-kin. Since I had no idea and even less desire to know where my stepfather could be found. She clucked some more and patted my hand. That hand was getting a lot of attention tonight when it was my head that needed it.

When she insisted on a name I gave her Shac's, then mentioned that he was currently a patient at the hospital. She frowned, but wrote his name down.

She took me to a tiny cubicle. So many pieces of equipment crowded it there was barely room for a bed. If I suffered from claustrophobia I would have been in even more misery. Another nurse came in and checked my vitals, pulse, temperature and blood pressure. And then for forty-five minutes I lounged on the narrow, hard bed. If my head wound had been critical my next stop would have been the morgue.

Finally a tall, tow-headed young doctor peered around the doorway, waved and said he'd see me in a moment. Five minutes later he came in, checked my head wound and wrote something on my chart.

"The bleeding has stopped. I don't believe stitches will be necessary." Pale sandy eyebrows climbed his forehead. "Unless you want me to sew a fine seam?"

"Just what every girl wants, stitches on her face. And another scar to go with this one." I pointed to my nose and the faint line down its bridge.

"Fall as a kid?"

"Not a fall, and I wasn't a kid." I replied.

"So – stitches? They'd be in the hairline."

"No, thanks. You can practice on the next homeless drunk who falls on a broken bottle."

He wrote something else on the chart. Probably 'patient refuses stitches against medical advice.' "I'll have the nurse put on a fresh dressing and we'll keep you overnight for observation."

"No way, doctor. As you probably have noted on your chart there, this patient has no insurance. And I'm not about to run up thousands in hospital charges I can't pay. I'll be eating bologna sandwiches for a year to pay this ER bill."

"You live alone. Sending you home with a head wound is not advisable."

"I'm going. So trot out your 'against medical advice' papers and I'll sign."

When I finally managed to leave the ER I went upstairs and watched through the stairwell door until my friend, Tabi Winters, was alone for a minute. I begged her to tell me where they'd put Shac after he'd been attacked earlier that night. Her supervisor called her to the med room to stock the cart for the next round of patient doses, so I scurried along the hall and turned left toward Shac's room.

I made it to his door and slipped inside. The bed closest to the door was empty, curtains drawn around the other one. Must not have had a private room available. The hospital normally didn't put roommates in with cops.

Just as I reached to pull the curtain aside enough to slip through, I heard a soft voice. "Honey, you're going to be all right. You have to be." I froze in place. A woman. Shac hadn't mentioned that he was seeing anyone recently. Someone, some woman, who would call him 'honey.' Who was she? Indecisive, I stood still for a few seconds.

No, by God. I had to see Shac, find out how badly he was hurt. If she was someone close to him, I'd leave after a few minutes, but I had to know.

The only light in the room came from the hooded night-light low on the wall. The figure that bent over Shac, hand caressing his forehead, jerked upright as I opened the curtain. She moved even closer against the bed, though she was already practically on top of him. "I thought it was a nurse. Who are you?" She asked in a flat voice.

"A - friend. I wanted to check on Shac."

Bushy brows lowered over wide-set eyes. In the shadows I couldn't tell what color they were. "I know who you are. That so-called private detective trying to get your claws into my husband."

Her husband. Hah. She'd divorced him for the vice president she thought was going places at Eastern Fabricators. Only when the company merged her plans were thwarted since all executives were out the door the same as me. Just recently I'd heard a rumor that Shac might be promoted to Captain of Detectives if Tawson retired. That was probably the only reason she wanted him back.

I ignored her ridiculous statement and managed to get a few words out. "I'm glad he's going to be all right." Then turned and left the room, head high.

Six

I paid the taxi with cash from the hospital ATM, giving him another five I couldn't afford to wait while I checked out my condo. I started up the walk wishing I had my Glock. I'd never considered the Wexler Pointe condo complex to be dangerous. At least from outside and even in the dark of night, though to be precise, it was now early Sunday morning. I'd noticed from the taxi a bank clock that gave the time as five-thirty a.m. The battery operated clock in my bedroom had read two-twenty when the rock came through my window.

My ex-husband had made it unsafe for me inside our home, even though my income made it possible for us to live there. When we got married he seemed to have come into some money. He'd dragged me to East Tennessee and paid a substantial down payment on the condo. But very shortly he informed me he was broke and I had to go to work.

He found an ad for a part-time worker at a garden center and insisted I take it. He worked there off and on, too, and contributed minimally to our living expenses. I got tired of hefting bags of mulch and fertilizer. After I'd worked at the garden center for a year and a half, I found a full-time job as a clerk in Security at Eastern Fabricators. Emory objected but since it paid more and he wanted to keep the condo he agreed.

The second year I was there, Tabi, who was then a nurse in the plant medical department. saw the bruises I tried to keep hidden. I didn't tell her that several times in the past neighbors had called police when they heard Emory knocking me around. She suggested I try for a transfer to a job as security officer in the department, knowing I'd receive training in self-defense. I did ask for the transfer and got it, to my surprise.

At home I remained the stereotypical abused wife, cowed, constantly trying to please. It took five years for me to build up to the determination to end Emory's iron control over me. My self-defense instructor, a kind volunteer at a women's shelter along with a serendipitous walk on Clare Creek Mountain finally got through to me and helped me see that I deserved better.

The ex and his minimal contributions to our household had ended almost two years ago. Three weeks after that executives and employees were laid off when Eastern Fabricators merged with an out-of-state company and almost everyone was replaced. My eight years, five as head of their security department, netted me a year's severance pay and my 401K, such as it was.

While at Eastern I had slowly and painfully acquired a degree of fitness, first with self-defense training from a former police instructor, then Tae Kwon Do classes, both without my husband's knowledge. That fitness had deteriorated during a mostly sedentary year as apprentice PI to Daniel Traynor after I lost my job.

Whether another year would find me still living at Wexler Pointe was an iffy proposition. In which case what happened to the spectacular view from my living room window would be moot, as far as my own pleasure went. But I was still determined to fight for the preservation of Clare Creek Mountain Park. It had probably saved my life.

Despite several roadblocks, including a broken arm when one of Daniel's clients pushed me down, I'd persevered in my goal to become a private eye. Even after my first client almost became my last. He killed the woman that he'd paid me to find, an exotic dancer, his estranged wife. I'd lain awake nights trying to bury regret for ever taking the case. And resisting second thoughts about my choice of career after being booted by Eastern.

In the end I decided to stick with my choice, which considering my current situation, in the crosshairs of a killer with a penchant for yellow roses, may or may not have been wise.

I forced myself to enter my condo, the taxi driver wouldn't wait long. I checked every room twice. Tested the strength of the plywood over the broken window, dismayed all over again when I saw the broken glass still littering my bedspread. Hopefully Maintenance would replace the window tomorrow. Unless they were backed up. I leaned out the front door and waved thanks to the taxi driver, who sped off immediately, car apparently already in gear.

I decided a cup of tea might relax me enough to sleep for a few hours. Maybe even reduce the dull headache that filled the right side of my head. I'd still had no medication for it, though the ER doctor did give me a prescription. To have it filled would have meant stopping at a twenty-four hour pharmacy, and I didn't know of one in Wexler Bend. I dunked a tea bag in a mug of boiling water and started to my bedroom. At the door I stopped. I couldn't tackle cleaning up the glass now, so I about-faced to the living room sofa.

My next cases after the wife-killer were run-of-the-mill bail-jumpers and suspicious spouses whose suspicions were often justified. Even a couple of small businesses availed themselves of my services. One wanted to find the ex-employee who ratted them out to the EPA over a small gasoline spill. And the other the accountant who skipped after helping herself to a few hundred dollars of company money to pay a department store bill. If I never again was retained in a problem that ended up becoming a felony criminal case it would be too soon.

I sat on the sofa, sipped tea, and considered the case involving the EPA informant. He had certainly been angry when I tracked down and identified him to his former employer. But only angry at me. He would have had no reason to murder two other women.

My thoughts veered again to Clare Creek Park. Wasn't the EPA involved in protecting wetlands? I would certainly think the marshes on Clare Creek Mountain qualified as wetlands. Why hadn't that been brought up at the Mountain Marsh Militia meeting last week?

And then my elusive memory clicked in.

The second murder victim. She was the leader of the group. Gloria - something. Had the police discovered that yet? Surely they had. I picked up the phone to call Shac and tell him. But what I'd seen in his room when I went up to check on him stopped my hand. The picture of him in his hospital bed, his ex-wife hovering, increased my headache ten fold.

I put the phone back on the cradle just as my doorbell rang. Maybe I should have the thing disconnected. Before I got to the door the bell rang again. I looked through the peephole to see a strange woman standing in the illumination of my now working porch light. Wait, maybe strange, but not unknown. I'd only got a glimpse of her in the dimness of Shac's room but this one had the same horsy face and upswept dark hair. I debated whether to open the door. What the hell. I swung it open and offered her a fake smile.

Seven

"What can I do for you?"

"We need to talk." She didn't return my fake smile so I let it go.

"Why?"

"I could stand here on your porch and we could discuss your stealing my husband if you don't care for your neighbor's knowing all about you."

Another internal debate. I hadn't stolen her husband and did I care if my neighbors heard our discussion. They already thought the worst about me, no doubt. I opted for privacy and swung the storm door open. She walked in, a triumphant look on her face, as though she'd won a round.

"Lady, I didn't —," I began.

"My name is Mrs. Shackleford Lane." She snapped. "Not 'lady.'"

"The ex Mrs. Shackleford Lane, I believe. More recently, Mrs. Nathan Taggert."

"We're working things out. Shac needs me now that he's injured because of you."

My overly sensitive conscience gave a twinge. I felt there was a grain of truth in her words. Hadn't I tried to salve my own feeling of guilt by telling myself Shac chose to stay here last night? I didn't ask him.

"Good for you. I hope you'll treat him better this time around."

I indicated the cup I still held. "Tea?"

She ignored the offer with a sneer. "Look who's talking. You've thrown over two husbands. I hardly think you're qualified for marriage counseling."

Let her think Shac had told me more than he had about their breakup. All I knew was that the woman was a company attorney who'd left Shac over two years ago and married the wimpy V-P who couldn't hold his liquor and got canned from Eastern Fabricators. Then she got an offer from a firm down state and they moved away. After she left Shac had studied hard for the Sergeant's Exam and passed the first time he took it. I glanced at her left hand.

No ring. She must have dumped the wimp and returned to Wexler Bend. And now wanted to win back the one she dumped first, Shac.

"I don't think you would have fared very well with either of my ex's. You'd probably be dead." *How did she know I'd been married twice? Shac didn't even know so he couldn't have told her.*

"And I don't think Shackleford would fare very well as Captain of Detectives with an ex-junkie - if it is ex - girlfriend."

I tried very hard to keep my expression blank. So she knew about my dependence on prescription painkillers. Again - how? It happened after Emory broke my jaw, soon after we'd come to Wexler Bend. And I kicked the habit cold turkey after I started work at Eastern. Random drug tests are a good motivator. Ah, the ex-V-P she'd married. Pillow talk?

When she opened the door to leave, light from the early morning sun bathed her in golden light. She turned back for a parting shot, hand on the storm door handle. "Leave my husband alone. You're not ruining his career." *Was the woman threatening me?*

After she left I sagged onto the sofa. Captain of Detectives. I supposed it would be natural to want to move on up in the department. But what about Captain Tawson? I'd heard some vague rumors, but hadn't given much credence to them. Was a shakeup about to happen in the Wexler Bend Police Department?

A nap had been impossible after the visit from the ex Mrs. Lane. Soon after I gave up the idea of sleep Shac rang the doorbell I hadn't yet disconnected. We sported matching bandages on our heads. Both on the right side. Apparently he'd convinced another reluctant hospital doctor to let him leave. I didn't ask him where he'd left the ex. I knew where she'd been half an hour ago.

Shac walked to my living room window and looked out. I knew what he was seeing. Tall pines, maple and sourwood trees in their spring green finery climbing the slopes of Clare Creek Mountain. I had never been able to decide if I most loved the sight in early morning or late afternoon light. My view included a bit of the marshes around the shoulder of the mountain that edged the reservoir. If Black Construction and their political action committee, *Free Enterprise Defenders-United for Progress*, or FED-UP, had their way my view would in the near future include several sprawling monuments to human greed and arrogance.

When he turned around, I took a deep breath and began talking. In the interest of full disclosure and cooperation with the police I made the mistake of telling him I'd attended a meeting of FED-UP's opposition group, *Mountain Marsh Militia.*

"Why?"

"Because I think Clare Creek Park is special, that's why. For God's sake, you grew up here, don't you think it is?"

"Sure it is. But that doesn't mean I'm going to join a bunch of tree huggers."

"Neither did I. I went to a meeting." I'd thought I was helping Shac's investigation by telling him that I'd seen Gloria Tejoso at the meeting. "Even tree huggers don't deserve to be murdered."

"Cam. Drop it. The development project is not a done deal. The Interior Committee can refuse to bring it to the floor. Complain to the Legislature. Or the city for turning the Park over to the state."

"Sure. I'll write to my state senator who's in bed with the developers who want to drain the marsh and put McMansions on it. Or maybe I'll go and see him to complain in person."

"To what end? You just said he's in bed with the developers."

"So? His ads say his door is always open to his constituents. I can certainly tell him what I think about the state ruining the Park."

"Forget the 'hail fellow, well met' personna. He's not a nice guy. Stay away from him."

I saw something in Shac's expression that chilled me. Surely a state legislator couldn't actually be dangerous to his own constituents. Right, and surely a father wouldn't tell his daughter her mother was a whore and would be better off dead. Just a few days before the mother did die.

I pushed down the thought. I'd failed to try and find justice for my mother. I wasn't going to fail now. Clare Creek Park had begun the healing of my soul. I wouldn't let it be destroyed without a fight.

After another glance out the window, Shac picked up the subject of the MMM meeting again, his official police detective face in place. "So you think Gloria Tejoso, the dam victim, was at a Marsh Militia meeting? Leader? Hanger on? Agitator?"

"I didn't say I 'thought'. I did see her. She seemed to be in charge. Maybe she'd found proof of Jarvis's misconduct. I guess it's possible Gloria's activism could be the motive for her murder. But what about the other woman?"

Shac was writing in his notebook. "About two weeks ago. Near the park entrance? How many people were there?"

"A couple dozen, I guess. Blue collar, white collar, outdoors types, hikers, maybe. And one of your guys was there. Didn't she take pictures?"

"Who? How do you know?"

"I don't know her name." I shrugged. "But I've seen her coming out of the station. Street clothes, detective or undercover cop, maybe."

"What was she doing?"

"Seemed to be memorizing faces. So why hasn't she come forward to say she saw Gloria? There are only a half dozen or so of you. Don't you know a little about what you're all working on?"

"Why haven't you told me this before?"

I didn't like his tone and my look must have told him so. "I only remembered after I got home tonight, - this morning - for your information."

His expression softened and the bandage on his head gave him an appealing look. "I know, It's been a hell of a night." He scribbled something else in his notebook.

"Her environmental activities may not be connected with her murder." I reminded him.

"We haven't ruled anything out yet. A customer from the bar may have had a beef with her."

"Both of the dead women received yellow roses at home, you said. I got yellow roses at home."

"But both of them worked at the same place." Shac said, tapping his pen as he went over his notes. "We're checking into all their activities. Was the other victim at the meeting?"

"I don't remember seeing her. It's possible."

"If you remember, you will report it, Cam."

"I told you about Gloria. You know I wouldn't hinder a police investigation." I gnawed a ragged fingernail and thought for a minute. "Where's Jarvis's office here in the District?"

"Out near the conference center." Shac's head came up. "Forget it, Cam. Don't even think about going to see him."

"Why not? He's my legislator, isn't he?"

"Stay away from him. I'm serious, Cam."

Eight

Shac's attempt to discourage me, to say the least, from going to see Senator Jarvis had instead made me more determined to pay the bastard a visit. At nine o'clock Monday morning I called the number for his office and his secretary, or so I thought, answered the phone. "Senator Jarvis's office, Laura."

I asked to speak with Senator Jarvis.

"May I have your name?"

"Cameron Locke."

"Are you a constituent?" Laura asked.

What difference did that make, I wondered. "Yes, I am a resident of Wexler Bend and therefore a constituent."

"Senator Jarvis is happy to visit with his constituents. But I'm sorry, he is not available at this time. I'll make an appointment for you, Ms. Locke."

"Well, I really need to talk to him, Laura. Are you his secretary? Do you know..."

Laura cut me off, a touch of frost in her voice. "I am Senator Jarvis's Personal Assistant. I'll put you down for May 15, Ms. Locke."

The line went dead. It seemed Laura did not share the Senator's happiness in hearing from his constituents.

I hung up my phone. So if the Senator was not in his office, he was either at home in his, or rather his wife's, river side estate or at the state capitol. Since the legislature was not in session this week, he might even be on a 'fact finding' junket somewhere.

The number for the Jarvis estate was not listed in the telephone directory. So I resorted to my computer and a database available to private detectives. I dialed the number

I found there. After about ten rings a musical voice with an accent answered. "Jarvis estate. Who is calling, please?"

"I'm Cameron Locke. May I speak with Senator Jarvis, please?"

"I am sorry. Senator Jarvis cannot come to the phone now. Message, please?"

"Thank you, no. I'll call a little later. Do you think he'll be available then?"

"I do not know. I will give him your name. Goodbye." For the second time I was hung up on and I had only dial tone in my ear.

She hadn't said he was not, maybe Jarvis was in town. I sat back in my chair, thinking. The other day when Rhoda Jarvis was found on Clare Creek Mountain, victim of an apparent attack, no statement was issued by the Senator. Which was sort of strange. You'd think he would be concerned about an assault on his wife. Then again the man did have a reputation as a womanizer and I knew for a fact that he was an abuser. The mystery was why the woman had gone back to him after her two week stay at the women's shelter.

I couldn't remember if I'd eaten anything since that peanut butter and banana sandwich late Saturday afternoon, which seemed an eon ago. An aide had given me a lukewarm soda while I waited in the cubicle at the hospital emergency room but nothing solid.

Oh, after Shac's ex practically shoved me from his third floor room, I dimly remembered picking up a chicken wrap at the Burger King near the hospital. Before taking that expensive cab ride in the Sunday dawn. Had I eaten it? Maybe not, since Louise Lane Taggert had barged in on me practically as soon as I reached home.

My vicious headache had made a smash-up of my memory of Sunday. The visit from Shac's ex who had as good as followed me, hadn't helped. Nor had his visit immediately after she left. After they'd both gone their ways I'd lain on the couch most of the day and night, dozing fitfully.

While I pondered what I would say to Senator Jarvis, if I saw him, I made a cup of the tea I'd offered to the ex-Mrs.

Lane and rummaged for some food. I didn't locate the chicken wrap from Burger King so I must have eaten it at some point in time.

My refrigerator held only two end slices of bread, a shriveled apple and a slice of cheese that had gone hard around the edges. A half sleeve of stale crackers completed my repast.

Now fortified somewhat I went to the bathroom to make sure I was presentable to call on my State Senator. I was glad I had. When I stood in front of the medicine cabinet mirror I saw that when the doctor bandaged my injured head, he hadn't bothered to wipe away all the blood. My friend, Tabi, a nurse on Shac's floor, hadn't mentioned it. I guess nurses and doctors are so used to the sight of blood they don't even see it. And when I got home I hadn't cared to go near a mirror.

I grabbed a washcloth and washed my face, paying close attention to the hairline and near the bandage. I glanced down at my clothes. Good grief. Blood speckled the crew neck of the tan shirt I'd worn Saturday and still was wearing when the EMS guys carted me to the hospital. Night before last? I must have really been out of it since I hadn't bothered to change clothes yesterday either.

I stripped the blood-spattered shirt off and found a clean one. At last I picked up my tote bag and left the condo.

I took the by-pass around town to Wexler Drive from the exit at the end of the bridge across Wexler Creek, which was really big enough to be called a river, and often was, when we had a rainy season. Wexler Drive followed the creek for three miles and then the Jarvis estate came into view. Which was actually the Shell estate, since it had belonged to Rhoda's family for generations. An ornate iron fence interspersed with substantial rock pillars surrounded the property. A quarter mile of paved driveway, bordered with manicured grass and artfully scattered flower beds, led to even more ornate tall gates which barred any further access to would-be visitors.

I had just reached the first of the row of matching willow trees which spread along the road on either side of the driveway entrance when I saw the gates begin to open Damn. If I'd been a little closer I might have managed to get through.

A small green car, an old VW, putt-putted through the gates when they had opened wide enough. Immediately they began to close again. I turned up the driveway and met the car about halfway to the gate. When I glanced toward the driver I felt as though a fist slammed into my solar plexus. Triggered by an actual memory. The driver of the VW was Emory Locke, who had punched me in the stomach more than once.

We both braked at the same time, staring at each other. My stomach muscles still cramped tight as a drum and my rate of breathing increased five fold. I was disgusted with myself. Inside my locked car Emory Locke could not get to me. And even if he did, I'd kicked his ass once, I could do it again. Besides this was a public road, well, almost. Emory had always preferred privacy when he indulged his cruel streak. Even so I glanced at the door lock to be positive it was engaged.

His window rolled down. A mocking smile parted his full lips. But in his eyes I saw a hint of the anger that was never far below the surface. "Maybe my sweet little wife is a somewhat decent detective if she found me. She'll be begging me to take her back before long."

"What the hell are you doing back in Wexler Bend?"

"Has lover boy been beating up on you again, Cam? Bandages always did become you."

"I wore enough of them when we lived together." I snapped.

"We were married, not 'lived together.' I had a right to keep my wife in line."

"Living in constant fear is not a marriage." I put my car in gear. What was I thinking, sparring with this misogynist.

"When we moved here I told you I had a reason and not to question me about it. Guess you didn't give up." His eyes had gone dark and dangerous looking. "Is that why you're following me?"

"Good God, I didn't even know you were back. I'm here because I want to talk to my state legislator. Hardly about you." But why was Emory here? Had he never left after all?

Before I raised my window a menacing expression crossed his face. "Some people have long memories. And money can buy a lot of revenge, Cam."

He popped the clutch of the VW and jerked down the drive. He probably considered that he was the winner of this unexpected encounter since he'd had the last word.

I sat there, car in gear, for a minute. Money. What did money have to do with Emory's presence in Wexler Bend?

Since Jarvis had owned the garden center where we'd both worked at one time, maybe Jarvis owed Emory some money. Or Emory had convinced himself Jarvis owed him money.

And revenge? Did Emory mean he harbored a deep desire for revenge against me because I'd escaped his hold? The only other person I knew who might want revenge against me was Bo McDonald, my stepfather. The man I suspected had killed my mother.

I drove on up to the ten foot gates embellished with scrolls and curving arches. A black box with two buttons along the bottom edge perched on a narrow stone pillar. I punched the one with a green light behind it. The same voice that had answered the phone earlier said, "Who there, please?"

"Cameron Locke, to see Senator Jarvis. It's very important."

"Senator Jarvis unable to see anyone. You go now."

"I really need to talk to the Senator. Please tell him I'm here."

"No. You go now." I heard a click and got no response to another plea for a meeting with the senator.

So the senator would not even explain why he couldn't see a constituent. Not that I was too surprised. I'd seen him once at an Eastern Fabricators function at the conference center.The only interest he'd shown in anything at the event appeared to be   feeling up the nearest well-endowed female. I reversed my car in the turnaround in front of the gates and made my way back down the driveway to Wexler Drive.

Nine

I thought about my encounter with Emory Locke as I drove back to Wexler Drive. I now knew where he was, at least right now. What about Bo McDonald? I had no idea where he was, possibly still in Georgia, possibly not. How could I find out? I could drive to Roswell County, Georgia and talk to Detective Jake Hunter, ask to look at the files. If Jake was still with the Roswell County Sheriff's office.

Why not? I looked at the dash clock. Ten-thirty in the morning. There was still time. I had no cases going at the moment. And I always carried a change of clothes, toothbrush and toothpaste along with extra undies in my tote bag.

So I accelerated back up Wexler Drive to the by-pass and took the exit on the other side of town to the Interstate. Early afternoon traffic on I-40 as far as Knoxville was light. It gradually picked up after the I-75 split and was as bad as usual from East Bank and Chattanooga and on into Georgia.

I made a pit stop at the large pretentious welcome center with its fancy peach logos. I made pretty good time on through the towns that had been wide places along the Interstate a few years ago. Now they sported long shopping strip malls and a few different carpet mills. Big New York name outlets, trying to get rid of their last years fails by selling them to the Southern yokels.

Cartersville's five or six exits marked the beginning of the really heavy load of vacationers headed for Florida beaches. Eighteen wheelers filled the right hand lanes ferrying the stuff that kept the country going. When they stopped, everything else would, too, eventually.

I stuck to the center lane, as usual, to avoid the speed demons in the left lane who thought limits didn't apply to them. And to stay out of the way of the drivers who dared someone to rear-end them when they zoomed into traffic from the access ramps. A brand new black Infiniti SUV loomed behind me, trying to intimidate me into moving to the right, which I couldn't because a Fed Ex tandem was currently occupying that space.

The wannabe NASCAR Danica on my left finally stopped talking on her phone long enough to move on and the Infiniti jumped over in front of a classic Mazda sport, who stood on his brakes and sat on his horn. The Mazda's rear tires smoked and I glimpsed the driver fighting the wheel as his car fishtailed and aimed for my front bumper. I jerked my foot from the gas pedal and hoped like hell he didn't slam my Corolla into FedEx. Fortunately he missed me by about three inches. I considered adding my horn to the bedlam but resisted the temptation.

A few miles later and I passed the exit that would have taken me to my grandparents farm near Fallon, a medium-small town in what used to be the boonies of Cobb County. My throat lumped up a little. If only Gram and Gramps could have lived longer. Maybe Mom wouldn't have moved us from the farm to Roswell. Maybe she wouldn't have married my stepfather and let him piss the farm away with his hare-brained get-rich-quick schemes.

Kennesaw University signs bloomed above the buildings on my right and then Barrett Parkway added more strings of fast moving cars to the already over loaded highway. Slung across the highway computer-generated signs loomed, advising the drivers hell-bent for downtown and other points south how many minutes it would take them to arrive. If they managed to get there.

Finally the exit for Roswell was next and I could start dreading my errand in earnest. Would they let me see the files? Or didn't it matter that I was the murder victim's daughter? No one from the Roswell PD had ever sent me any updates on the case after I moved to Tennessee. At least I'd never seen any. Now that I had faced up to the diabolical lengths an abusive spouse would go, I wondered if Emory Locke was the reason I never saw any reports. If there had been updates and he'd gotten to them first and kept them from me.

Traffic lights on the surface streets to what used to be the small town of Roswell, Georgia barely kept traffic moving at a brisk walking pace. Having been swallowed by Metro Atlanta many years ago Roswell was a mere bump in the sprawling urban blight that was now the city. Would there even be any records kept in the old police station. Or new one, if one had been built. Maybe it was all electronic now. I probably should have called ahead.

At last I spied the red brick building and it still had *Roswell Police Department* etched across the wide marble strip along the front. I pulled into a visitor slot and sat for a minute. Wondered if Detective Hunter was still on the job or had retired. He'd been gruff but kind, unlike his female partner, who seemed not the least concerned that I believed my stepfather had killed my mother.

Ten

The large lobby seemed filled with people though they probably only numbered a hundred or so. Chairs lined the outer wall. Some people filled out forms balanced awkwardly on purses or backpacks. Others talked on cell phones or shouted at each other to be heard. A couple of uniformed officers behind a high desk seemed to be fighting a losing battle to keep some kind of order in the chaos. I walked up and waited to be noticed. Finally the older officer, Sergeant stripes on his sleeve, looked at me. "Help you, miss?"

"I'd like to talk to Detective Hunter, if he's still here?" I tried to pitch my voice loud enough for him to hear me.

"Hunter? Yeah, he's still here." He picked up a phone. "May be out. Tell him who wants 'im?"

"Cameron Locke. Well, he'd know me as Cameron Parsons. He worked my mother's murder case several years ago."

Something flickered in his eyes. I wondered if he remembered it. I didn't remember him, but he was probably here at the time.

He turned away and spoke into the phone. I couldn't hear what he said until he turned back and repeated it into the phone while looking a question at me. "Cameron Parsons? Yeah. Her mother was a murder victim few years ago."

I nodded. I was glad Hunter was still here and at the station. Maybe I could head back after looking at the files and get home before midnight. If Hunter let me look at the files. I crossed my fingers behind my back.

The Sergeant put his phone on the cradle and told me to find a seat. Hunter would be out as soon as he could.

I thanked him and looked around. Seeing no empty seats I wandered around the lobby. I wound up at one of the big front windows and stared at the steady traffic streaming by outside. Across the street was a building with neon signs advertising the presence of several bail bond offices. Location, location, location, as the real estate people say.

This area had gone steadily down hill for years until those who could escape the festering inner city began moving further and further out. Gentrification followed as surely as day followed night. But crime followed affluence just as surely. Hence still the need for this police station and bail bondsmen.

My ruminations were interrrupted when I heard my name over the din in the room. I turned and saw a face I still remembered, though more lines bisected the broad forehead and Hunter's dark hair now showed more streaks of gray. His striped shirt was rumpled but he still stood straight as a board, remnants of his days as a Marine. He saw me at the same time and began maneuvering toward me.

We shook hands and he said, "This way, Miss Parsons. Or, you got married didn't you?"

"Yes. It's Locke, now. But I got divorced, too. Should have taken my name back."

He nodded and led me through a pair of steel doors. We had to wait a few seconds to be buzzed through another door. About halfway down a long hall, he walked through a wide doorway into a room that in spite of its size seemed crammed with desks. Thirty or forty crowded the floor in pairs, backed up to each other. There hadn't been as many here twelve years ago. But Hunter's was still in the same place, back in a corner, and still piled with stacks of folders, loose papers, pens and a cardboard coffee cup, half full. He pulled out a chair and motioned for me to sit. No partner seemed to be around, I really hoped the sameness of his workplace didn't extend to his partner.

"Coffee?" He asked before he sat in his chair.

"No, thanks." I glimpsed the shield lying next to a report on the desk and saw that it now read 'Sergeant' instead of just 'Detective', and added, "Sergeant Hunter."

A faint nod acknowledged my noticing the promotion. "What can I do for you, Ms. Locke?"

I smiled. He really was kind to me before. "Call me 'Cam,' for one thing. And I came down from Tennessee for a specific reason."

"Which is –?"

"I want to see the files and reports of my mother's murder case."

He didn't say anything for a moment. "It was a long time ago, Cam. And we never actually classified it a murder case, you know. Why now?"

"I don't even know if any progress has been made on finding how exactly my mother died. Did you find any evidence that pointed to McDonald at all?"

Hunter fiddled with some papers, tapping them on the desk, aligning them evenly. "I know you said at the time you were certain he was connected with her death. Do you still think so?"

"Oh, yes. Did you?"

"Has he contacted you since then?"

I frowned. "Contacted me? No. Why?"

"Bo McDonald is in Federal Prison in Atlanta. You didn't know?"

"How could I?" I heard my voice rise and tried to tone it down. "I've heard nothing at all about the case. Shouldn't I have been notified about the trial?"

Hunter waved a hand to calm me down. It was his turn to frown. "I got your note about your marriage. Just couldn't remember the new name at first. I've sent messages every year updating you. Didn't you get them?"

"Messages? No, I didn't. And I'm sure it's one more thing my ex did to isolate me. Which is why he's now ex." In Hunter's eyes I saw something before he blinked and it was gone. I knew what it was. The knowledge that daughters of battered mothers often also married abusers.

I gripped the strap of my bag, wishing it was Emory's neck. "So, he must have been found guilty of something in Mom's death?"

Hunter was shaking his head. What the hell? Why was McDonald in prison then? "So why is he in prison?"

"We never found any evidence that pointed to him for sure in your mother's death. He was convicted of another crime and sentenced to fifty years to life. He'll never bother you again."

Thank God. Or whoever. Then Hunter's last sentence registered. 'He'll never bother you again.' With slight emphasis on the 'you.' But I'd never told him or anyone except my mother that her husband had tried to rape me while she was at work. I was sure she had confronted him and that's why he killed her. And I'd carried the guilt of that certainty with me ever since. If she hadn't found the courage to defend me, though not herself, would she still be alive? I'd never know.

Hunter appeared to be waiting for me to return to the present. When I did, he nodded and continued speaking. "After you left town, a young woman came to the station. He was her father, married to her mother, whom he also abused, even when she was dying of cancer. He molested and raped the daughter repeatedly. When the girl was almost eighteen, the mother died. The girl ran away to a relative, who finally persuaded her to report her father's crimes. She and others testified. He was found guilty and the jury gave him fifty to life. One juror told the press she wished the death penalty had been an option."

My shock must have showed on my face. Hunter reached to pat my hand. I'm sure he wondered if I'd also been raped. I'm equally sure it was only a matter of time if I hadn't told my mother about the attempt.

"So you never heard about the case?" Hunter asked.

"No, as you've no doubt surmised, I married a man very much like my stepfather." I shuddered. "Thankfully, we had no children. But until the last couple of years, I had no mental or physical energy to look into Mom's death."

"Look into?" Hunter gave me a quizzical look.

I backpedaled quickly. "Even think about it. I grieved a long time, of course. But my priority was staying alive. And trying to be 'good enough.'" I sketched quotation marks with my hands. "So my husband wouldn't feel the need to 'correct me' with his fists."

Hunter had worked with enough battered women to know what I meant. He nodded. "So how long have you been divorced? Ex leave you alone?"

"He left Wexler Bend after I kicked him out, literally. I just found out today that he's back."

"Wexler Bend, Tennessee." Hunter snapped his fingers. "Yeah, that's where your note said you were moving to."

A thought occurred to me. "When did you first send me an update?"

"About six months after you left. Why?"

I didn't really want to go into it. But what the hell? "That's about when Emory's emotional abuse and bullying first escalated to really beating me up."

Hunter just shook his head. "How long has he been gone?"

"About eighteen months." But was he really gone from my life? I couldn't help wondering now that I knew he was back in Wexler Bend. I wasn't sure I wanted to go into the murders of the young women and Shac and Captain Tawson's suspicions.

"Just like that?" I couldn't blame Hunter for the skepticism he tried to hide. Few battered wives just up and threw off their abusers. Especially not the ones on their second long-term abusive relationship. Many ended up in a coffin like my Mom.

"Not exactly." I admitted. "I had help after I landed a job in a plant security department and took some self-defense training courses. Even then it took a while. A few years later I lost the job, but I'm thankful for the time I had it."

"That gives me great satisfaction to hear, Cam. If you don't mind me saying so."

I shrugged. "Of course not. You were kind. Is your partner working today?"

He laughed. Had probably followed my thought progression. "Gone on to bigger and better things. Chief of Detectives down in a small city near Savannah."

"Good for her. I'll be sure to avoid it."

"Don't feel too hard toward her, if you can help it. She went through some bad times herself and she built a tough shell around her emotions."

I shrugged again. I'd been twenty-five when Mom was killed driving home late at night from her job at a fast food joint. The steering on her old car went out and it went over an embankment.

I knew when I opened the door to my dingy, dilapidated efficiency apartment and saw the uniforms it was bad news. I also knew my stereotypical wicked stepfather was most likely the cause. But Jake and his department could find no evidence. Other than the fact McDonald came by my place and threatened Mom if she didn't forget about me and my problems and come back to him.

Hunter looked at his watch. "Hey, why don't we grab some lunch. Give me a minute and I'll print out some reports about the trial, if you like."

"Please do. I need to know."

"Wait here. When I come back we'll go out the side entrance and avoid the madhouse out front."

So I sat beside his desk and looked around the detective squad room. It was certainly a lot bigger than the one in Wexler Bend. Shac had taken me through the station there when I still hoped I'd have a job with the department. Here in Roswell there were several female detectives sitting at desks, working on their computers or talking on the phone. Through a glass partition I saw an attractive olive skinned woman sitting at her desk. Stenciled on her door was her name and title, "Lieutenant Patrice Consolo." She looked out toward the squad room, saw me staring and a small smile pulled up the corner of her full lips.

Just then Hunter returned as I nodded and returned her smile. He pulled his jacket on and handed me a fat manila envelope. "She's okay, as Lieutenants go." He nodded toward the glass partition. "Transferred in last year."

We left the squad room by a door at the back of the room and walked down a short hallway to an outside door which led to the official vehicle parking lot. We stopped at a nondescript dusty brown Ford halfway across the lot. The interior of the vehicle was worn but clean and the seatbelts not too twisted.

"Burger King okay? It's nearby and I have an appointment in an hour."

"Sure. Anywhere." I was trying to decide how much to reveal to Hunter about my life. Most regular police detectives didn't care a lot for private eyes. If I told him I was now a licensed PI he might not be too forthcoming and I wanted more information.

"Are you convinced he didn't kill my mother?" I asked him after we'd ordered our burgers and found a booth. I didn't think I needed to clarify who I meant.

Hunter bit into his double patty burger and chewed for a minute. "I can't say."

My expression must have revealed my thoughts a little too clearly for he waved a hand. "Don't get me wrong. We talked to people. They knew what was going on, what kind of man he was."

"Oh, yeah. But they couldn't be bothered to help." I knew I sounded bitter. Bitterness twisted my gut.

"I agree, he is certainly capable." Hunter went on. "But there just wasn't any evidence to be found that he'd tampered with the steering on her car."

I dipped a fry in the ketchup and tried to chew it. It felt like tomato-flavored rubber in my mouth. "I wanted to kill him. I knew he did it and he knew it. And I could see him laughing inside."

"Cam." He waited for me to look up. "He won't be getting out. He's already had to be put in isolation several times. He hasn't changed and one day another prisoner may actually get to him."

"If I talked to him, do you suppose he'd tell me?" I hadn't realized I was going to ask the question, but there it was.

Hunter stared at me in astonishment. "You want to go see the bastard?"

"No, I don't want to see the bastard!" I said, too loudly. Several people glanced up, then back down at their food. I lowered my voice and continued. "But I want to know if he killed her because she promised to support me when I filed charges against him."

"I strongly advise against it." Hunter said. "He's a master manipulator. You know that."

"And I've already demonstrated that I'm susceptible to manipulation, right?" I said through gritted teeth.

I could see his jaw set as he tried to find the right words to avoid agreeing with me and to convince me not to go to the prison. "You've begun making a good life for yourself. You got a new life, didn't allow losing your job to send you looking for another strong but abusing male figure. Let it go, Cam."

Eleven

My hand froze in midair as I started to dip another fry into the ketchup. "You ran a background check on me while you were getting the reports."

He had the grace to look a little shamefaced. "I'm a cop. It's what I do."

The look in his eyes reminded me of Shac when he found the two wilted roses in my kitchen trash – what? – just a couple of days ago. He had the same 'determined to protect Cam, whether she wants it or not' look. Shac displayed it when he squatted down, reached inside my kitchen trash can and pulled out the yellow rose I'd found on the porch earlier, holding it carefully by the stem end.

Shac had dug through my trash for the roses because he was worried about my safety. Why was Hunter worried about me visiting my stepfather in prison? What could the son of a bitch tell me that was worse than what I already suspected?

"Why?" I challenged him.

"Why?" I challenged him.

"Why what?" Hunter took the last bite of his sandwich and a long drag of his drink as he eyed me with fake lack of understanding of what I was asking.

"Why shouldn't I visit my – the bastard? What's he going to tell me that you don't want me to hear?"

"Who knows what he'll say? Manipulators can spot a vulnerability to exploit without even trying."

I pushed down the memory of what happened when my first abusive husband was knifed to death in jail after I finally filed a complaint. Mom had scolded me for not choosing a husband more wisely than she had – and I'd finally told her what a real bastard she had married. She'd found the courage to face my stepfather, for my sake, and two weeks later she was dead. "And you think I'm still vulnerable?"

He wadded up his trash with more vehemence than really necessary. "Look. I'm off tomorrow. I'll go out to the prison with you."

"No. Tell me."

Hunter slid out of the booth and said, "Come on."

I followed him out to his car. *What did he have in mind?*

After we got in, he pointed to the manila envelope. "Read the top report. Now."

I stared at him for a minute. He waited. So I pulled up the clip and took out the thick sheaf of papers. By the date on it, they were in chronological order, the first one being most recent. It was the transcript of McDonald's final interrogation before he was charged with the assault and rape of his daughter. I scanned down the page.

"Detective Hunter: ...you raped your own daughter?

McDonald, suspect: Hell, no, she wanted it. She's always coming on to me.

Detective Hunter: When she begged you to stop, you refused.

McDonald, suspect: She never. She liked it, I told you.

Detective Hunter: She says she begged you to stop. Said she'd tell her mother.

McDonald, suspect: Liar. Just like that cunt stepdaughter of mine. Both liars.

Detective Hunter: So you raped your stepdaughter, too?

McDonald, suspect: No. They both wanted it. Sluts, like their slut mamas."

My hand crumpled the paper and I balled it up. Son of a bitch. That's why Hunter looked at me like that. The son of a bitch told Hunter he'd raped me.

Hunter started to touch my shoulder, was smarter than Shac and thought better of it. He gripped the wheel and tightened his lips, avoided looking at me.

"He didn't, you know. Rape me. I came home to my apartment and he was there. Mom was still at work, though he said she was home. He grabbed me in the kitchen and I managed to get loose. My blouse tore and I pulled the dish cupboard down in front of him. A broken plate cut his arm, I saw blood spurt high in the air and I got away."

"So that's where he got that long scar. He wouldn't say."

He looked at his watch and sighed, in relief, it seemed to me. By then it was too late to call about driving to the prison to see the s.o.b. So Hunter said he'd call the prison early in the morning. I took a room at a Motel 6 and told him to let me know what time and I'd be ready when he picked me up. Only to learn that when he called the bastard was in solitary confinement and could not have visitors. With no reason to remain in Georgia I headed back to Tennessee.

Twelve

Daniel Traynor opened his office door. He looked surprised and not real happy when he realized who his early evening visitor was. "Cam. Haven't seen you for a while. What brings you out here on a foggy night?"

"I was in Georgia for a couple days."

I'd known Daniel since third grade back in Fallon. The class nerd, he was always called Daniel, never Dan. He even escorted me to the Senior Prom, though we separated just inside the door and I didn't see him again the whole night. I was told he got laid for the first time by the so-called 'easy' girl in our class after a few drinks out in the parking lot.

We graduated. A couple of years later I married the first guy who asked me, a womanizing sadist who'd apparently studied under my stepfather. The marriage ended less than a year later through no effort of mine. The husband of a woman he was sleeping with stabbed him when they were both in county lockup.

Daniel earned an associate's degree from the local community college and did a stint in the National Guard as an MP. He actually married the girl from prom night, but it only lasted for a couple years. He'd never remarried though I knew for a fact it wasn't from a lack of willing women.

While in the National Guard his unit did a training camp in East Tennessee and he liked the area. So he moved to Wexler Bend after he left the Guard, got a license and put out his shingle as a Private Investigator. It must pay okay, his home was in a nice subdivision on the edge of town. Who would have guessed that my own second venture into matrimony would bring me to Wexler Bend and back in contact with Daniel.

Daniel closed the door and led the way into his home office. A large fish aquarium was against one wall. It's aerator gurgled but the tank contained no fish. He said he stopped trying to keep them, he was gone from home so much. "Coffee? Just made a fresh pot."

"Sure. No cream." Daniel could remember the license plate number of a philandering husband he'd tailed five years ago but could never remember how I took my coffee.

While he got the coffee from his nearby mini-kitchen I sat down in the chair he reserved for visitors and glanced at his computer screen. A form was on the screen. I glimpsed the name in one of the blanks just as his screensaver kicked on. A collage of images swirled back and forth across the screen, binoculars, a camera with long-range lens, a panoramic microphone. I stared at the mesmerizing display and wondered if I'd seen what I thought I had seen.

"Were you near our old stomping grounds in Georgia?" Daniel walked over with two cups of his signature strong aromatic coffee.

"Roswell County? Yeah. Needed to check on some things."

"Oh?" He sipped his scalding coffee.

I blew on mine, stalling for time. Had I really seen the name I thought I had on his computer form?

I cast around for something to say. Daniel might not know about the attack on Shac and the rock through my condo window. "Somebody threw a rock through a window at my condo a couple of days ago. I wondered if I pissed somebody off recently, to use Shac's phrase, or if it was from an old grudge."

"Like Bo McDonald, your stepfather? Isn't he in prison?"

I was looking down at my coffee, blowing on it again. I hoped he couldn't see enough of my averted face to see my shock. My breath stalled and I felt like I'd just been sucker punched in one of my self-defense classes. I had to answer so I forced in some air and raised my head, took a sip of coffee. I pantomimed a quick breath and trying to swallow hot coffee.

"Ooh. Yes, he is. I was going to see him but he's in solitary. So it couldn't have been him heaving rocks through my window."

"Were you badly hurt? I noticed the bandage by your ear." Daniel had a concerned look on his face but I knew him well enough to see the wariness in his eyes. Had he realized I'd caught his slip of the tongue? How and for what reason would he know my stepfather was in prison?

Inside I was pretty devastated. Daniel was my oldest friend in Wexler Bend, or anywhere. I counted on him. I couldn't believe he was holding back secrets that concerned me. I had been certain he was a straight arrow, as straight as Shac Lane, and that money couldn't buy his loyalty. Daniel had taken me on as an apprentice he didn't need, at minimal pay, for the year the state of Tennessee required. And steered me toward the required classes I needed to qualify for a Private Investigator license.

The Wexler Bend Police Department, my first choice, had posted a job opening soon after my layoff from Eastern Fabricators. I'd done extra workouts at the gym in order to pass the physical. Before I learned that thirty-six was just past maximum age of thirty-five to be considered for the job.

Detective Shac Lane had plied me with beer and tried to convince me I was better off missing the chance to be shot or stabbed by criminals or angry spouses or run down by irate motorists. He'd taken me to a higher class bar than usual to console me, the Clare View Hotel lounge.

"Hey, get your license and become a Private Eye."

"Huh? I wouldn't know where to start." I drained my second bottle and Shac signaled the attractive blonde bartender for another.

"So, talk to Daniel Traynor. Ask him how to get started."

Through the beer buzz I tried to think about talking to Daniel. PI work was mostly cerebral, wasn't it? Tapping computer keys and looking up facts at the library. I'd never have to chase down a perp or defend myself or someone else against an armed lunatic. Maybe it would be preferable to being shot at.

"Maybe I will." I didn't know if it was the beer talking or if I really would talk to Daniel. I was disappointed about the non-job with Wexler Bend Police, but still a little touched with euphoria that I had actually sent Emory Locke packing. My walk on Clare Creek Mountain had been the final catalyst propelling me to freedom.

I'd gone to the mountain so fearful, depressed and disgusted with myself I wanted to get lost in the woods.

I walked at random through the undergrowth, oblivious to low-hanging branches scraping my face and arms. And I had come upon this patch of gaily blooming yellow roses amid random bits of rock foundation. Why had they hung on for - how many years - with no one tending them? If they could cling to life in such a hostile environment, and produce this beauty, I ought to try and do as much. This much beauty I was unlikely to produce, but I could at least attempt a life worth living. Maybe I'd move to Florida. Become a snowbird.

After I met with Daniel Traynor I asked him to call a buddy in Pensacola to feel out the possibility of getting into the business there. His buddy didn't think it a good idea. Said PI's were all over the place, backstabbing each other, though not him, of course, to get clients. So I'd stayed in Wexler Bend and I had been glad I'd stayed, on the whole. But with Shac's ex now back in the picture and standing between us, if I couldn't count on my old friend from Georgia to have my back, who could I count on?

Gloria Tejoso picked up her travel bag, purse and laptop case. She surveyed the empty living room, bereft of any evidence that she had lived here. All the furniture sold or given to Peter. She wondered how long his live-in fiancée would let him keep it. Didn't matter to Gloria, he was her problem now. When you dated and won a married man, what did you have? A man who cheated on his wife. At thirty-two Gloria had now learned that hard lesson personally. Grandma Elena had warned her, but she refused to listen. She figured it must be in the genes. Her own biological mother had made the same mistake.

In Grandma's letter she said that the company which owned the hotel had paid a substantial settlement after Teresa's death in the mass shooting. Grandma had put part of it into a trust account for Gloria. Gloria never told Peter about the money for some reason. Added to her share of the proceeds from selling the house and almost all her possessions and the lump sum payment from Peter, she could afford to search for her mother. Though she suspected her mother was probably one of the party girls killed in the shooting. The irony was not lost on her. Her birth mother and adopted mothers both dying in the same tragic event.

For months she'd been undecided whether to stay on in the house she'd shared with her philandering husband. The tabloid picture of her mother and the Tennessee State Senator she found at the newspaper archive had made up her mind. She'd sell the house, take that money and her inheritance and marital settlement and move to Tennessee.

Thirteen

I realized I'd been too long in answering Daniel's question. I reached up to touch the bandage I'd just replaced before driving to Daniel's and made a rueful face. I was supposed to have gone back to the hospital for that but I couldn't see paying hundreds of dollars for a few inches of gauze. "Not really. It was the window behind my bed. The rock grazed me."

"Did the police find who did it?" Daniel's solicitous expression really looked genuine. "Any idea why or was it a random act of violence?"

"Not yet. I suppose they're still trying to find out." He didn't ask about Shac. I wondered if Daniel even knew about the attack on him. I wasn't about to volunteer any information until I had some idea what Daniel was doing working for Senator Jarvis. For that was the name on the billing invoice I'd glimpsed on his computer just before the screensaver came on.

I decided to do a little questioning myself. "So, are you working on anything interesting?"

Daniel's gaze just barely started to move toward his computer before he caught himself. He shrugged. "The usual sleaze and money lifts. Kind of human failings that keep us PI's in business. Yourself?"

It was my turn to shrug. Maybe if I put out a feeler he'd let something slip. "I'm sure you know about the recent murders of young women, body of one found up in the park?"

"Sure. Unusual for this small burg. Shac tell you if they've found any evidence pointing to the murderer?"

"He's pretty close-lipped about ongoing cases."

He nodded. "The park seems to have a lot going on up there lately. Do you know if they think the Senator's wife being kidnapped and left there by the MMM has anything to do with the murders?"

Was Daniel's question a little too casual? He set his cup down on a coaster, picked it up again. Took a sip.

"Other than chastising me for having anything to do with the MMM, he hasn't said much about it."

"You joined the MMM?" The surprise in Daniel's voice was genuine. He knew I was not a joiner. Of environmental groups or any other kind.

"No, I didn't join." I didn't hide my irritation. "I attended a meeting. Wanted to see if it looked like they were going to be able to do anything to stop the development up there."

"I know you love the park. The view of the golden maples and red sourwoods from your condo is pretty spectacular in the fall." Daniel's expression of empathy seemed a little forced.

His description of my view brought back my last conversation with Shac before I left for Georgia.

"The hell you say. You joined one of those crazy environmental groups?" Shac had hurled the words at me that evening.

The second murder victim was the leader of the Militia. I was Shac's source for that fact, but I hadn't seen a newspaper since I'd been back in Wexler Bend. Maybe the police hadn't released the information. If they had, why hadn't Daniel mentioned it? I hated these questioning thoughts about Daniel. But all my life experiences had taught me one thing. Don't trust anybody.

"I do love it. And the view is the only reason I kept the condo after Emory left."

"Or you kicked his ass out." Was there a new sharpness in Daniel's muddy brown gaze? "Do you know where he is now?"

Why had he jumped on the subject of Emory Locke's whereabouts? To distract me from my possible glimpse of his invoice billing Senator Jarvis? What had he done or what was he doing for the amoral state senator? Shac and I had

had words about him, too. I'd wondered if Gloria's murder was tied to development in the park.

Shac had warned me to stay away from Senator Jarvis. And now it appeared that my oldest friend and mentor was working for the guy. I ignored his question and he didn't repeat it. We talked about inconsequential things for a few more minutes. I made an excuse, left his office and went home.

I trudged from the parking lot toward my condo, stopping en route to check my mailbox. It bulged with junk mail and I'd only been gone one night. Any longer and I'd have needed more than the extras I carried in my tote bag. My decision to stay overnight in Roswell County and let Detective Sergeant Hunter drive me to the federal prison in Atlanta had been all for nothing as it turned out since my non-beloved stepfather was yet again confined to solitary confinement and denied visitors. I wasn't sure if I was glad or not. I certainly had not looked forward to seeing his sorry face. Reading his statement had been enough of a blow. I still wasn't sure if Hunter believed the son of a bitch hadn't actually raped me, though given more time he would have found a way, I was sure.

Hunter said he'd go over the case, or cases, again and get in touch with me if anything occurred to him. I wasn't going to hold my breath. I thought I'd detected a touch of non-police-work interest in the way he looked at me when he pressed his card in my hand. Maybe a long-distance semi-relationship would be easier to handle than my current local semi-relationship with Detective Sergeant Shackleford Lane. Though if I was smart I'd forego any kind of relationship with any man. I was pretty well convinced none of them could be trusted after my visit with Daniel Traynor.

I'd thought I could trust Shac. I met him the first time a neighbor called the police. I'd known Emory was OCD. He always meticulously arranged boxes of foodstuffs according to height. For some reason I'd forgotten and set a box of cereal between two taller ones in the kitchen cabinet. The first time I did it Emory slapped me. The next time he knocked me through the front window of the condo just as the neighbor was walking past with her dog. She screamed and dialed 911 on her cell phone. I refused to go to the hospital or press charges against Emory. Shac did his best to change my mind, but I wouldn't in spite of the pain and blood on my face from multiple glass cuts. By good fortune only, most were superficial and healed without scarring except for the one on my nose.

Later Emory threatened to kill the neighbor's dog. In fact though when he kicked at it one day and it growled he jumped back about ten feet. "Goddam dangerous animal. Animal Services will take care of you."

Next day a For Sale sign was in front of her condo. "Guess I showed her." Emory crowed.

Maybe I'd get a dog, too. Dogs were usually loyal to their human friends. Even male dogs. I opened my front door and went on through the living room to drop my tote in the mess that was still my bedroom. The sight depressed me even more. At least glass was in the window again, instead of plywood. The drapes lying across the bed partly covered the broken glass still there. Maintenance obviously considered glass removal, except from the window itself, was beneath them.

Fourteen

The message light was blinking on my phone. I pressed the button and deleted half a dozen hang-up calls, probably telemarketing calls, never mind that my number was on the state's Do Not Call list. Then I heard Shac's voice. "Cam, pick up, I need to talk to you." Then again, "Cam, where the hell are you? I really need to talk to you."

Just as I deleted Shac's voice on the third call demanding to know my whereabouts, as if the answering machine could tell him, my doorbell rang. As soon as it stopped, it rang again. And again, one long ongoing ring before I could get to the door. I knew it had to be Shac, no one bent on harming me would ring the bell off the door frame. I jerked it open and stood glaring at him. "I refuse to sprint to my front door. For God's sake, give a person time to get here."

"About time you got home. You could have had complications from your head injury and be lying inside unconscious. I was about to break the door down."

"Like hell! I've just now got my window repaired. Do you want to bankrupt me with homeowner fines?"

He stepped over the threshold and I had to either back up or be walked over. "Please, come in, Shac. Unexpected guests are such a pleasure." If he picked up on the sarcasm he shrugged it off.

"I've been trying to get you all day."

"Obviously. I just listened to your many messages."

"Where were you anyway."

"If you must know, I was in Georgia. Overnight."

"Georgia? Why?"

"I don't want to go into it right now. I'm exhausted."

"I have to tell you something. I didn't want to tell you over the phone. Sit down."

"What is it that's so important you had to barge into my house? I'm tired. As you mentioned, I was attacked and injured yesterday, or the day before, whichever."

He led me to my easy chair and gently pushed me down on the seat. Then pulled the small straight chair, only thing I had that had belonged to my mother, away from the wall and sat on the edge.

Now I felt a touch of uneasiness. This wasn't the Shac I was used to dealing with lately. He'd been kind and gentle each time he'd been on duty when the domestic disturbance calls to my home had come in. But since I kicked Emory out he'd been a supportive but mostly impersonal friend.

"What? Has there been another murder victim? Who?"

"We're not sure. If it's murder, I mean. Probably, though it's not another woman. Cam, it's Emory Locke. His body was found at the base of the dam at Clare Creek Reservoir this morning. But two yellow roses were nearby, like the other victims."

Of all the things that had raced through my brain in the last few seconds, this was not one. "Emory? Emory Locke, my ex? How ... what?"

"You told Captain Tawson you thought he was in Florida. But when he checked with the PD in Miami they said he was no longer there. Had he been in touch with you?"

"Of course not." He hadn't been in touch with me. On purpose anyway. "He wouldn't dare." I snapped.

I didn't like the implications of Shac's question. Did the police think I'd pushed Emory over the dam? If I'd been up there with him, it would have been tempting, but I hadn't. And besides I was three hundred miles south when it happened apparently.

"Cam. I'm sorry, but we need an official identification. We haven't found any relatives yet. Do you think - ?"

My stomach clinched and the chaotic thoughts running wild in my head froze abruptly. "You want me to identify him? Seriously?"

"We have to have one. If you can't, I'm sure we can find a neighbor, or co-worker at the garden center to do it."

They could do that. I didn't have to look at the dead face of the man who had made my life a living hell for more than six years. The law couldn't compel me to do it.

I unclenched my hands and sighed. Told myself to breathe. Emory Locke couldn't hurt me anymore. Even more certainly than my bastard stepfather couldn't. Maybe it would be good for me to look at him, to know that finally, deep in my soul. "Okay. When?"

Shac searched my face for several minutes. Dark green eyes sending a message I wasn't sure I saw, or wanted to see. "You don't have to, you know."

"I know. Maybe it will be good for me. When?"

"It could wait until morning, if you want. We're sure it's him. Identification is just a formality."

I stood up. Tried to hide the fact my knees were a little shaky. I should have known I couldn't hide it from Shac. He took hold of my elbow and held it until I was steady. "No. Let's get it over with."

I went to the bedroom and picked up my tote bag, first removing the soiled socks and underwear from my Georgia trip, told myself to remember to replace them.

Shac drove me to police headquarters. Wexler Bend didn't have an actual morgue with refrigerated compartments. The county leased space in the local hospital, a fact not generally known. For actual autopsies bodies were shipped to the state capital.

But identification via closed circuit visuals made it unnecessary for anyone to go to the hospital facility. We walked to the detective squad room and to Shac's desk. He dialed into the morgue's closed video circuit and turned the monitor of his computer toward me. "Ready?"

"As I'll ever be." I managed.

He touched a button and there was my late ex-husband's battered face in front of me. Gone was the sneering cruel smirk on his full lips. The image more nearly resembled the shocked unbelieving look he'd worn when I stood on his back after I'd kicked his ass to the floor. I could see dark bruises and abrasions all over his face, though it had been cleaned up. I wondered what had gone through his mind in those seconds he was falling. If he had been conscious, that is. Did he regret the things he'd done?

I was certain I wasn't the only woman he'd knocked around. Could a man like him ever acknowledge even to himself that he'd done awful things? Personally, from all my life experiences with men like Emory and my mother's husband, I doubted they did. But who had pushed him? I could not even begin to imagine he had jumped out of remorse for the things he'd done. A thought occurred to me.

I looked at Shac and he clicked the picture off. "Do you identify the victim as your ex husband, Cam?"

"Yes." I said, voice steady as I could make it. "It's him. Emory Locke."

I waited until he'd made a notation on a form. "Shac?"

He looked up. "Does Emory's death, murder, whatever it is, knock a hole in your serial killer case?"

He didn't say anything for a moment. My mind went back to the night in my kitchen when he showed me the pictures of the two female victims. I couldn't help shuddering.

I pushed those pictures to the back of my mind. Maybe those young women were just random victims of different killers. And now Emory's death a third random death by violence. Or accident? Neither seemed probable. In a small city like Wexler Bend, surely that was not a likely statistic.

Shac took so long answering my question I wondered if he was going to answer. Apparently his thoughts were running along the same lines as mine. "Don't know. We don't even know if he was killed or if he fell. Different type of victim, if he was killed. Different motive, maybe. Damned strange to have a string of three suspicious deaths in a burg the size of Wexler Bend though."

"Three victims – two of them at the dam? Surely there has to be a connection." I was too tired to think clearly.

I'd made the abortive trip to the Roswell Police station after my encounter with Emory on the Jarvis driveway. Oh, Lord, I hadn't filled Shac in about that.

Then I'd not been able to go to the prison to talk to my stepfather after staying overnight in Georgia. My early breakfast with Sergeant Hunter, the long drive home, my unsettling visit with Daniel Traynor and then learning about Emory's death had left me feeling as though I'd been dropped off the dam myself.

"Four victims. Are you forgetting you're an actual and potential victim yourself, Cam?" Shac brought my thoughts back to the present.

That brought my adrenaline back up. "I am not a victim!" I said, grinding my teeth.

"Cool it." He shot back. "You do remember the yellow roses and the rock through your condo window?"

"So, Sergeant, who wants to hurt me then? The only two I'm aware of who would are either in the morgue or in prison."

"I suppose you were with people in Georgia?"

He asked the question so softly I almost missed the implication. When I did, I jumped up from the chair. "You think I might have pushed Emory over the dam?"

"I have to ask, Cam. You know that."

"And I would not be sorry if I had pushed him. But, yes, indeed, I was with people. A Homicide Detective Sergeant Hunter in Roswell County, actually. Satisfied?"

"The whole time? All night?" His voice was expressionless.

"No, of course not. I checked in at Motel 6 on Roswell Road at six p.m. yesterday and met Detective Hunter at seven a.m. Tuesday, this morning. I suppose I could have made the round trip back here in that time, but I didn't."

I made an about face and marched toward the door of the squad room. I heard him coming behind me. "I'll take a taxi home. You don't need to bother."

"I'm driving you. Live with it."

The only sound in the car all the way to my condo was the muted police radio. To my surprise Shac didn't ask any more about my trip to Georgia. Or why I was with a homicide detective.

A suspicion surfaced in my mind. Had Hunter called Wexler Bend and talked to Shac so he knew all about it? From the corner of my eye I could see that he, too, still sported a bandage on the side of his head. It was smaller than his original. I wondered if his bitch of an ex had replaced it.

The thoughts I harbored about Shac's ex-wife were no more charitable than hers about me. After I'd left the ER against the doctor's advice and checked on Shac, she'd followed me home.

Her possessive words in the hospital and later at my condo told me she felt I was a threat to her efforts to get close to Shac again. She had no idea how resistant I was to another relationship with any man. I couldn't believe Shac had designs on me either, so why was he always in my face?

Fifteen

I expected Shac to let me out in front of my condo. But he got out of the car and managed to get to my front door ahead of me. "Your key." He ordered.

"What do you think you're doing? I can open my own door, thank you."

"You're not going in until I check it out. Give."

I considered refusing, but decided it wasn't worth it. I handed over my key. He unlocked the door and reached in to turn off the alarm. I waited, not patiently, while he went through the rooms, weapon in hand, turning on lights as he went.

He called, "Clear."

I walked inside and stood pointedly near the door. "Thank you. Now please go so I can go to bed."

"Set the alarm. Keep your gun close." He instructed, looking me in the eye.

"Yes. Yes. I'll be fine. Goodnight." I closed the door behind him and reset the alarm. Reached into my tote bag and touched my Glock.

my condo Saturday night, then sabotaged the electricity to my house and flung a rock through my bedroom window. Was it only two days ago? And what, if any, was the connection with my late un-lamented ex-husband?

Emory's face swam before my mind's eye. Not as the image on the morgue computer screen an hour ago, but his menacing look and words as he drove down the Jarvis driveway. Then I remembered. Shac's accusing question out of left field had driven from my mind the thought of mentioning my encounter with Emory.

Could it have been Emory outside my condo throwing rocks that night? Who had slammed something hard against Shac's head? If so, why was he lying dead in the morgue now? Did he have anything to do with the deaths of those two young women? Again, why? Now that Emory himself was dead maybe the question was moot.

Emory, my second husband, dead, like my first. Maybe I was some sort of black widow. No, I refused to accept that. I was not the bad guy in my marriages.

My thoughts went reeling back to the day I'd freed myself from the suffocating hold Emory held on me.

He was waiting for me when I walked in the door of our condo after that walk on the mountain. His even features were relaxed and his lips curved in a smile as he lounged against the kitchen counter. It didn't reach his light blue eyes. "Where has my little wife been this afternoon?"

I wanted to turn around and run back up the mountain. My heart pounded and my mouth dried up. I swallowed. "I went up to Clare Creek Park and walked around." My voice started to quaver and through a mental fog of fear I ordered it to stop.

His eyes narrowed and lips thinned. "Walked around?"

"I needed to get out. We had a stressful situation at work."

"Really? Stressful situation?" He put a mocking quality into the words. "Oh my."

"An employee heard rumors about a layoff and brought a gun to work. He didn't want to give it up."

"Did he put those scratches on you? Did you two have fun in the woods, darling?"

I shrugged out of my backpack and put it on the floor. "I'll start dinner."

"Oh, so now you think I might want dinner prepared by my harlot wife?"

"I don't know why you say that, Emory. You know I've been faithful to you."

"Do I?" He suddenly stepped toward me and swung his right fist at my face.

My thoughts went reeling back to the day I'd freed myself from the suffocating hold Emory held on me.

He landed on the kitchen tiles, hard. I would have laughed at the shocked look on his face, but the adrenaline I willed to kick in finally did. I had to rein in the fury it produced so I wouldn't make a foolish move. Emory didn't rein in his anger. He leapt to his feet and came at me.

I easily sidestepped his charge again and grabbed his left arm, twisting it behind his back, kicked his feet from under him. This time when he landed I jumped on his back with both boots.

He screamed, there's no other word for it. "Bitch. You broke my back. I'll kill you."

"No, you've hit me for the last time." I knelt on his back, got my arm around his neck and twisted.

"Just a little more pressure and you'll be the one dead. It's over, Emory. Do you understand?" I pressed a little harder and he tried to scream but it came out as more of a gurgle.

I jumped off and waited to see if he wanted to continue the battle. But the fight was all out of him. As usual with bullies, he was ready to call it quits when his victim fought back.

Zeb Glaston, former police training officer and my self-defense instructor had told me he would. But I knew he had worried that I wasn't determined enough to escape Emory Locke's iron hold. Even when he heard that I'd subdued a couple of guys bigger than me in my job as Security Chief at Eastern. Zeb had worked with enough abused wives to know the odds that I would get away from Emory and stick to it, though he'd trained me well. The fact we didn't have kids gave me a little bit of an edge. The rest was strictly up to me.

"Pack your things and go shack up with the slut I saw you with at Hooters."

He stopped trying to get to his feet and glared up at me. "What?"

"Don't even try to deny it. Just go."

He left that day. I was placing half a dozen of the yellow roses from Clare Creek Mountain in a vase as he walked out. His venomous look would have dropped me on the spot if possible.

I'd asked Daniel Traynor to try and find out if Emory was still in town. He had moved in with the blonde sleaze I'd seen him with, but the copy of my divorce petition the lawyer sent to him at her place came back 'addressee unknown.'

We published it in the Wexler Chronicle and a few months later our divorce was final. Losing my job weeks after I finally defied Emory could have caused me to doubt my inner change, but I hung onto my new self-image as a woman able to take care of myself. And by God I would.

Since then I'd not seen him until …. And I still hadn't told Shac about seeing Emory at the Jarvis estate.

Sixteen

I finally forced myself to fold the bedspread on my bed around the broken glass still on it. Since it was one I'd used when Emory was still in my life, I decided to ditch it. I'd get a new one at the discount store downtown. I vacuumed the sheets and the carpet around the bed then replaced the sheets. By the time I was finished I decided to shower and go to bed even if it was only ten o'clock.

After a night when no alarm blaring or rocks through a window woke me, I made a pot of coffee and dressed in jeans and long sleeved shirt. I hadn't mentioned to Shac that I planned to go up on the mountain. He would have forbade me or failing that have insisted he had to be with me. It was a crime scene, yada yada yada.

I wanted to look over the area at the base of the reservoir dam where Gloria Tejoso's body had been found. And now Emory had died there also.

I knew there were light years of difference between the motivation for Shac's actions and my stepfather's and Emory's beatings. But he had brought back those memories that I'd already relived enough times recently, the day I finally stood up to my abusive husband. Cup half way to my mouth, I froze.

Emory knew I loved yellow roses. I'd assured Shac and Captain Tawson that Emory Locke was a wife-abuser, not a cold-blooded murderer. Was I right? Could he have murdered those two young women? Why? And why was he now dead? Did he have an accomplice? The thought sent a coldness down my spine.

I shook off such thoughts but did make sure my Glock was still in my tote before I left my condo. The washout that had closed the road for weeks had been repaired, I noticed, as I rounded the last bend before the gate at the park entrance.

Fern Huff, the park employee who'd manned the gate for years, waved me on through. The sticker on my windshield identified me as a Park Friend. My annual dues gave me unlimited access to the park during the hours it was open. I made a mental note to stop and talk to her on my way out. Though I knew the police would have already questioned her about the times of the deaths at the dam.

The road wound on through the woods to the parking area between the Planetarium and Nature Preserve. The dam and reservoir were to the left of the Planetarium about a quarter mile. But my destination at the moment was the site of the old homestead in the other direction. I wanted to see again the blooming perennial roses that still stubbornly hung on around the foundations of the long-gone habitation.

I parked and set out along the asphalt trail that looked so out-of-place among the hardwood trees, smooth green-leaved laurel and rhododendron bushes. No wind stirred the new spring leaves overhead as I walked.

The undergrowth thinned somewhat as I approached the homestead site and I caught a glimpse of sunny yellow through the trees. I'd known they were still there as late as last fall. Blooms on the bushes began to open in early summer and continued with abandon until first frost. I dropped to the ground next to a bush with dozens of the dewy yellow roses among its pointy leaves, just as I had that other visit to the Park. Several blossoms had layers edged with brown wilt and were past their prime but some looked so fresh they might have only opened that morning. And among them were dozens of tightly wound buds waiting their turn to open their petaled hearts.

I owed my present mostly-free-of-fear life to these lovely examples of tenacity. Why had several of them been used as precursors to the murder of young women? Could those roses actually have come from these hardy bushes?

The day I found them I began to shed my life as the abused daughter who grew up to be a punching bag for two husbands. I'd held a responsible job, had enough training in self-defense, but not the will to free myself from the second husband, Emory Locke. No more. The Cameron Locke who came down off the mountain from Clare Creek Park the day I stood up to Emory was not the same woman who had climbed it. I was determined to keep it that way.

When I returned to the parking lot I sat for a few minutes in my car, thinking. Was it simply coincidence that Rhoda Jarvis had been abducted and left in the park? No motive and no names of possible abductors had been released by the police. And why had she returned to her abusive husband after fleeing to the women's shelter? I assumed she had since the news story had not included any reference to an estrangement.

On Saturday the news anchor had mentioned a conference Rhoda Jarvis was scheduled to address Wednesday, this evening, at the Clare View Hotel Conference Center. The occasion was the annual meeting of the Women's Service Club of Wexler Bend, the organization that funded and provided much of the everyday operating expenses for the women's shelter. Rhoda had assured the anchor she would certainly still speak to the group despite her ordeal.

I'd had occasion to visit the conference center in the past, though not as a guest, at one of the fancy parties it often hosted. Eastern Fabricators had rented the ballroom several times and spent a fortune on banquets for top executives and as many local dignitaries as could wangle an invitation. They had me bring along a couple of guys from plant security to keep them safe, though the conference center had a small security force. Nothing ever marred the drunken good times they enjoyed except the occasional upchuck from the VP of Operations, notorious for his inability to handle his liquor. More than once he'd stumbled out of the hotel hanging onto the woman who'd married him thinking he was on his way up the corporate ladder, Shac's ex-wife.

Seventeen

At six-thirty I drove around the winding drive to the rear of the Center and parked. In the reddish painted back wall the door to the Security Office looked like all the other doors of varying width except for a small green star in the upper right corner. I banged on it and a couple minutes later it was opened by Zoey, one of the officers I'd worked with at Eastern before she left to head security at the conference center. A tweezed eyebrow rose up her smooth mocha forehead when she saw who it was.

"Cam, didn't expect you."

"Hi, Zoey. Got a minute?" I tried to smile as though we'd seen each other just last week instead of a year ago.

She pulled the door wider and grinned. "Sure. If you're not here to try and get my job since Eastern closed its doors."

"Got one." I pulled out my Private Investigator license.

She took the folder and looked closely at the card inside. "Cool. Never saw one of these."

I took it back and stowed it in my tote. "Me either until I got it. Only takes a year working for a pittance and another Private Eye vouching for you."

Her dark eyes showed a touch of alarm. "Are you looking for someone? You're not here to hassle a guest, are you?"

"No. No." I crossed my fingers behind me. I couldn't think of a backup story if Zoey didn't swallow the crap one I was about to feed her. "I'm checking the layout for a prospective client. A wannabe-celebrity rapper. Just signed a tour contract. He's been asked to do a benefit concert here and he's worried about security." I shrugged. "Perfectly good, I assured him. Even so I said I'd see if anything had changed since I worked Security for Eastern."

"Who is it? Someone I know?" Zoey was enamored of all things rap. I'd made up a name but hoped she'd buy that it was confidential right now.

"Doubt it. He's from out-of-state, caught a lucky break."

A couple of frown lines creased her forehead. "I might have heard of him. Tell me."

I tried a regretful expression. "Sorry, Zoey. Since he's not committed yet, he didn't want me to disclose it."

"Wel-l-l-l." She looked around the tiny office then glanced at the walkie-talkie on her belt. "I'm alone until Darrell gets back from supper. But I'll walk you around a little. Most concerts are held in the big ballroom, but we got some kind of ladies meeting going on in it right now."

"Great. Thanks, Zoey."

Probably one hundred fifty women milled around the conference room as Zoey and I entered. Five more were on the dais, a couple sitting, the other three chatting near the end of the table. Six chairs were at the table, four unoccupied. Just then a young woman led an older one up the steps at the end of the dais. The older woman had auburn hair and when she turned to look out over the room I saw that it was Mrs. Jarvis. I should have known. How was I going to get to her?

I started down the aisle between rows of tables. Zoey grabbed my arm and yanked me back. "Are you tryin' to get me fired, Cam?" She hissed.

"I have to talk to her." Several seated ladies turned toward us, frowns marring the makeup ad-ready faces beneath hair fresh from salons.

Zoey's fingers dug into my arm and she dragged me back through the double doors. For a petite young woman from Alabama she was strong. She swung me around and got in my face. "Cam. You will not disrupt this meeting." She emphasized each word with a finger in my chest.

I raised my hands, palms out. "OK. I get it. I won't disrupt the meeting."

She did a smart about face and took my arm again, none too gently. She walked me back down the corridor, through her office and all but gave me the bum's rush through the door. I caught a glimpse of Darrell behind the desk, mouth and eyes wide open, just before the door slammed shut with me on the outside.

"Crap." I marched to my car, got in and sat there thinking. The dinner meeting was to last from seven until ten o'clock. My dashboard clock showed about eight-thirty. I drove around the building and parked in the second row from the entrance that served the restaurant and conference center. At nine-twenty-five I went inside and ask the restaurant hostess to seat me at a table on the side. A velvet rope separated those tables from the stretch of lobby the dinner attendees would take when they left the corridor leading from the conference room to the exit. I was taking a chance that Zoey would spot me, but I meant to speak to Rhoda Jarvis. A server took my order for coffee and I pulled out my notebook, sitting with my head down.

How had Rhoda Jarvis got on the mountain? Somebody took her in a car? What did they say to her? I jotted down other questions while keeping one eye on the hallway from the conference room. At a little after ten several of the sets of double doors opened. Women straggled through and began walking toward the exit.

I dropped a five on the table and strolled from the restaurant trying to keep a casual eye on the women. A few milled around the lobby, but Rhoda Jarvis still hadn't come out. Had she left another way? I made my way against the tide and finally spotted her near a doorway. A tall woman in a dark silk suit and raven hair piled high on her head was deep in conversation with her. Jarvis held up her right wrist, checking her diamond encrusted watch. I got the impression she was anxious to get away from the woman.

"Call me tomorrow, Evelyn. We'll talk." Jarvis patted the woman's arm and turned away. Since I was standing less than a foot away, she almost collided with me and her one-of-a-kind *de la Mer* bag slipped off her right shoulder. "Excuse me." She glared, yanking it back up.

"Mrs. Jarvis. May I have a moment?" I held my ground.

Eighteen

I started after her just as Zoey grabbed my arm and twisted it behind me. The training we'd both gone through was good. I was at a disadvantage because I didn't want to hurt Zoey. She, on the other hand, apparently had no such inhibitions.

"Don't even think about it!" Her voice was low and mean but perfectly clear. "I should have you arrested for trespassing, Cam."

All the women had now left the corridor, a couple glancing back apprehensively. I pulled loose from Zoey's hold, not without effort. "No grounds and you know it. This is a public space."

"Mrs. Jarvis could charge you with harassment." Zoey said.

"She won't."

The certainty in my voice seemed to stop whatever answer Zoey was going to give to that. Her brown eyes filled with curiosity. "Why not?"

"She has reasons." I rubbed my shoulder to let Zoey know she had hurt me. It didn't faze her.

"You're fine." She offered. "Go home and put the heating pad on it. How do you know she won't file charges?"

I remembered something I'd meant to ask Zoey earlier. "You must have known one or both of the two young women murdered recently? One was a hostess in the restaurant here."

Zoey blinked at the sudden change of subject. "Yes. Everybody's in shock, we liked them both."

"Not everybody, I guess. Do you know anybody who'd want to harm either one?" I watched her expressive eyes but saw no hint of deception in them. Zoey was honest to a fault.

She found it almost impossible to tell a little white lie, much less a big one. Not always a trait you found in a security guard but it worked for her.

She couldn't hide it when something occurred to her now. Her pretty lips pursed in a small 'o.'

"What?"

"It's nothing," she said. "I forgot to tell Detective Lane about her boyfriend."

"What about him?"

Zoey hesitated. "I'd better call him. He said if anything else came to mind to let him know."

I made a show of looking at my watch. "I'm meeting him in half an hour. I'll tell him and he can call you to get it in your own words." I had little hesitation in telling big lies myself. Besides I would tell him. Sometime.

"Well. Candy had a boyfriend, I think he may even have come to town when she did. But he never came around here. A very private person, she said. A couple of days before she died, she mentioned that he kept asking her about people who stayed at the hotel and who worked here."

"Did she seem worried that he might hurt her or something?" I asked.

Zoey shook her head. "I don't know. Not really, I guess, or she'd surely have stopped seeing him." She glanced at me guiltily. She knew my history. "Or maybe not."

I touched her shoulder to show her I wasn't offended. I didn't want this flow of information to dry up. "Do you know what he looked like?"

She shook her dark short curls again. "Like I said, he never came around. She showed me a picture on her cell phone though. Said he didn't know she'd taken it, would be angry if he found out. Smooth, good-looking, but I'd say he was several years older than Candy."

"Hair? Eyes? Height?"

"Blond. Pale blue eyes. Cold. He was not much taller than Candy, five six or seven, maybe. I don't think he cared as much for Candy as she did him."

"Thanks, Zoey. I'm sorry she's dead. She didn't deserve what happened."

"No." Zoey sighed. "I better get back to work. Bye, Cam."

I left the conference center and was walking toward my car when it hit me. Zoey had just given me a decent description of Emory Locke. Zoey had only worked for Eastern Fabricators security for little more than a year. I was pretty sure I'd never shown her a picture of Emory. My shame had prevented it. Could Emory have been Candy's secretive boyfriend? And now they were both dead. The rain showers that had been threatening all day chose that moment to start falling. I dashed for my car.

Nineteen

I approached my condo with more caution than ever. I parked in my designated space, which was not immediately in front due to a jog in the curb to accommodate a fire hydrant. Its presence was the reason we'd been able to afford the place. Emory Locke was dead. But if he had been working with someone else, which didn't seem likely, I wasn't taking a chance. Once inside I set the alarm and set my tote bag on the desk in my office alcove. The shrill peal of the doorbell made me jump a foot. The shoulder Zoey had yanked behind my back and my rock-damaged head zapped instant complaints to my brain.

I stomped back to the door and put my eye to the peep hole. "Might have known." I growled, threw off the lock and jerked the door open. "Am I to expect nightly visits from now on?" Only after the words left my mouth did I realize how they sounded.

"Good evening to you, Cam." Shac didn't seem to notice what I'd said. He removed his jacket and shook raindrops from it as he draped it over a chair. Then went to lean against the kitchen counter, arms crossed.

"Why are you here?" I walked around the counter.

Shac looked toward the coffeepot. I took the hint and pulled out the coffee canister, filters, flipped the switch on the Bunn. When I turned back to the counter he had picked up the two photographs I'd never given back to him.

"Someone found another body?"

"I believe you are supposed to tell me something." I tried to look away from his dark green gaze, failed. Damn Zoey and her honesty. She must have called him after I left her.

"If you already know…" I shrugged.

"Don't give me that, Cam. You still swear you didn't know Emory was back in Wexler Bend?"

"Well, he obviously didn't want me to know."

"Knowing him, I would have thought he'd want you to know, taunt you. Wouldn't you?"

"Well, he didn't. What do you think happened? Is there a connection?"

"I don't know. None of it makes sense. We've found no connection between the two women. No evidence that the girl from the conference center restaurant was at the MMM meeting. They moved in different circles."

"And neither moved in my circle." I paused in front of the open cabinet as I reached for a mug.

"What?" Shac pounced. I needed some lessons in not telegraphing my thoughts.

"Except that one meeting. How long had Candy worked at the conference center restaurant?" I handed him the mug with a handcuff graphic on the side I'd ordered from a catalog.

He set the mug down and pulled out his notebook, flipping pages. "Less than a year. Why?"

"I thought if she was there when I worked for Eastern I might have seen her at one of their functions."

"So, not. Since you left Eastern nearly two years ago."

"Nicely put. Since I was canned, you mean."

"Not the only one. And you've landed on your feet. Don't be so hard on yourself."

Why was Shac buttering me up? I didn't know anything else to tell him.

Wrong, I learned from his next question. Evidently Zoey had told him everything she'd told me. "Did Zoey's description of the boyfriend sound familiar to you?"

I had to admit it had occurred to me. "He must have been deluded enough to think I'd care if he dated someone. And I'm sorry the poor girl got involved with him."

"Maybe she reminded him of you." My face must have shown the recoil I felt. He put his arm up in mock defense of his head. "Not that you're in any way responsible. You know that."

"Was she just another conquest then? Did he kill her and Gloria Tejoso? But why Tejoso? Then what happened to him? Took another woman up there and fell himself? And she's afraid to come forward?"

Shac looked at me. I could have sworn I saw respect in his eyes. "You might have made a competent police detective, Cam."

To cover my confusion I picked up the two photographs he'd laid back down. Gloria and Candy. Somehow knowing their names made it more horrible. Two pretty women struck down in their youth. How had they threatened someone enough that it cost them their lives? Was Emory their killer? I prayed not.

Shac drained his coffee mug and stood up. After pulling on his jacket he turned toward me and opened his mouth.

I held up my hand. "I know. Lock the door, set the alarm. I got it."

"That, too. But I was going to say, I'll talk to your friend, Zoey, in the morning. If she calls you with anything else she's remembered, call me. Cam?"

"I will, I will. With friends like you and Zoey, who needs enemies?" I was sorry the minute the words were out of my mouth, but I couldn't call them back. His eyes seemed to shutter. He walked to the door and left, but closed it gently, which was somehow worse than slamming it. And I still hadn't told him about seeing Emory at the Jarvis estate before I left for Georgia.

I put our mugs in the dishwasher, emptied the coffee carafe and went to shower and brush my teeth. When I crossed the bedroom to my bed my big toe found a piece of glass in the carpet the vacuum cleaner had missed. I swore and limped back to the bathroom for a band aid.

Reminded of the terror I'd felt that night the rock shattered my window, grazed my head and landed on my bed, I was too wide awake to sleep. So I flopped in my office chair and pulled out a legal pad. If I went over everything and wrote it down my subconscious would pop something out. I hoped. First I began to just doodle as usual.

Twenty

I began with the two yellow roses left on my porch, for no obvious reason. Then Shac bringing the pictures of the two female murder victims and telling me they'd also received the yellow roses. My yellow roses had looked very much like the ones I'd found on Clare Creek Mountain at the old homestead. I had no way of knowing if the roses the two young women received were the same. Had I mentioned the roses on the mountain to Shac? I made a note to tell him.

Under the names of the women I made a list of the facts as I knew them. Gloria Tejoso, blonde, bartender. Was that what had tickled my memory, I'd seen her working the bar at the Clare View? But I'd only been in that bar once, with Shac, and apparently even he didn't remember her. She worked nights, lived with fiancé (name? Find out), killed on Clare Creek Mountain. Candy Cohrn, single, hostess in conference center restaurant, worked mornings, found by neighbor (name? Find out), possibly girlfriend/lover of Emory Locke, no family. Rhoda Jarvis, left bound to a tree on the mountain. Cam Locke, me, recipient of two yellow roses, attacked in my home but still alive and kicking as was R. Jarvis. But a few days later Emory Locke found dead on the mountain at the base of the reservoir dam, two yellow roses nearby on the ground. The only commonalty among us, as far as I could see were the yellow roses. The roses were in the park on the mountain. Gloria's and Emory's dead bodies were found on the mountain, but R. Jarvis was found alive there.

I shivered as a memory swam up. On several occasions when I'd visited the old home site on the mountain I'd sensed a presence. I'd attributed the feeling to a fancy that the long ago residents of the farm were glad someone appreciated their place after all the time it had been abandoned. Maybe the woman who'd planted the long lived rose bushes. But could it have been a present flesh and blood person? Hiding somewhere nearby in the woods, watching me? Why? I glanced toward my front door and the reassuring steady green light on the security panel. I turned the pad over and laid my pen on it. Decided to leave the small desk light on and went back to my bedroom and climbed into bed.

Reflected sunlight off the next condo building streamed through the now bare window above my bed when a long peal of my doorbell woke me. Again. The bedside clock joined in and claimed the time was nine a.m. I threw the covers off and stalked toward the front door as the bell gave another long note. Of course, when I put my eye to the peep hole I saw that it was Shac. Again. Wearing a different nicely pressed shirt and minus the bandage on his head. Courtesy of the ex, I wondered? Back in his bed and board?

I flung the door open and turned to walk to the kitchen without saying a word. The door closed and I assumed he had followed me to the kitchen. After I pressed the switch on the Bunn I faced him across the counter. "What now? Not everyone gets up at the crack of dawn."

"Obviously." His gaze traveled down my ancient red and white polka dot pajamas. I couldn't throw them out because their much-washed softness was so comfortable. A hint of amusement hid in the green depths of his eyes. Then he sobered. "Emory told you he had no family, right?"

"Yes. Said his parents died when he was young. They had had no siblings and neither did he. Why?"

"He lied. Big surprise. Guess who shares, or shared, his DNA?"

I nearly dropped the mug of coffee I was handing to him. "What? Who?"

I nearly dropped the mug of coffee I was handing to him. "What? Who?"

"Our bartender victim. Same blood type, A negative. His in AFIS from his run-ins with the law, of course. Hers from when she worked for a company doing business with the US government. Both almost identical." He looked at me and waited.

"Almost identical? How can that be?"

"The 'almost', of course, is that they were male and female. So, fraternal."

"Twins? For God's sake. He must have known."

Shac reached for the sugar bowl and stirred two teaspoons of sugar in his coffee. He sat on a stool and took a swallow, added half a spoon more. "Maybe. He never gave a hint that he did?"

"No. He walked into the diner in Fallon where I worked and struck up a conversation. I was lonely. Made the mistake of accepting a date and married him even though he was the same type as the first guy I married against Mom's advice. He never talked about any family, in Georgia or here in Wexler Bend."

"Did he give you any reason for moving to Wexler Bend?"

I'd wondered about that myself. "No. But as I learned more about the psychology of abusers I figured he was just taking me away from everything I'd known, any friends."

"Probably that, too. We've been digging back into the victim's lives. Gloria Tejoso grew up in a community in metro Atlanta. Her original birth certificate shows she was born in a home for unwed mothers near Roswell and adopted by a Hispanic family."

"New Hope Center." I breathed.

He nodded. "Her certificate shows that she was a twin, but apparently the mother kept the other, a boy."

I could hardly take it in. Emory born at New Hope Center, one of a set of twins born to a mother who didn't want both babies. Twins have a special connection to each other. Had he known or suspected he was a twin? How could a mother just walk away from one of her children and keep the other? Did Emory resent that his mother deprived him of his sister? Who was their mother? I looked across the counter at Shac. He'd apparently been following my train of thought.

"Don't know yet who's their mother. If she's still alive, even. She seems to have disappeared after leaving New Hope with Emory three days after the births."

"What name did she give?"

"Tejoso. Elizabeth Tejoso."

"So she had already made arrangements for the adoption." Another thought leapt to mind. "Or were the birth mother and adoptive mother the same person? To cover up an affair, maybe?"

"No. She'd already made arrangements for the private adoption when she arrived at New Hope, nine months pregnant, unaware she was carrying twins."

"And decided to keep one. So where did Emory grow up? He was back in Roswell when I met him."

"His mother evidently changed her mind and gave him up for adoption before he was a year old. Something happened and he was raised in foster care. Brace yourself for another shock."

Had anything Emory told me been the truth? Had his mother cared for him? Did he know who and where she was but told me she was dead?

I needed sustenance to take all this in and went to the cabinet. Pulling down a box of shredded wheat I poured some in a bowl. Looked at Shac and raised my eyebrows. He shook his head. I took my Almond Breeze milk from the refrigerator and poured it over the shredded wheat. Returning to the counter I got a spoon from the drawer and took a bite.

Shac's last words echoed in my brain, 'another shock.' "What's this other shock?"

"Emory was a fellow inmate at the county lockup where your first husband was killed."

Shock was a mild word for the tsunami that swept over me. "Say what?"

"Actually they were in the same holding cell the night your husband was stabbed."

I felt dizzy with all the thoughts whirling and colliding through my mind. And their implications. "But – are you

96

saying Emory might have had something to do with Mart's death?"

"Another inmate actually stabbed him. A couple of the others in the cell claimed they believed Emory incited the stabbing someway though."

"Why? They didn't even know each other."

"As far as we've been able to find out, no, they didn't." But Shac's eyes weren't meeting mine suddenly. What was he keeping back?

"Why was Emory in lockup? He never told me he'd been arrested."

"Altercation at a bar. He assaulted the bartender."

"The bartender?" I thought of Gloria, the first murder victim. It was hard to think of her as Emory's sister. Twin sister.

Shac shook his head. "No. Not his sister. But it was a female. Lieutenant – uh, Roswell police haven't unearthed the reason for the assault."

I pretended not to notice his slip. He had probably talked to Detective Sergeant Hunter. After all, it was his jurisdiction. If I found out they'd discussed me in a personal way though there was going to be hell to pay. I stirred my cereal around the bowl, remembering those years I would rather have forgotten.

Twenty-One

After my Dad died Mom married Bo McDonald, who had a bad reputation around town. I was so angry with her. We'd moved to the farm near Fallon where she grew up and I wanted us to stay. I felt safe and loved there, working with Grandma in her vegetable garden. Long beds of Georgia's abundant canna lilies edged her front yard. In the fall we dug up and thinned the tubers so the tall big-leaved plants would produce even more abundant scarlet blooms the next spring.

Grandpa was warm and loving, not cold and detached like my father, who couldn't even be bothered to think of a name for his newborn daughter. Mom was nearly full-term with me when they'd driven to a town named Cameron near the Georgia coast. To visit relatives, friends, vacation? I never knew why. She went into labor, which lasted for hours and finally I was born in the tiny hospital there. When asked what I was to be named my father just turned his back. Exhausted, Mom told the nurse, "Just put down 'Cameron' as her name."

When I was ten Dad developed fast-growing cancer in his lungs and died when I was twelve. McDonald came around, telling Mom how beautiful she was, he was going to take care of her. After they married he moved us back to Roswell and the physical abuse began. He'd come home and if he didn't like the smell of the food she'd prepared, he knocked her across the kitchen. Once he held her arm an inch from the gas flame. The ugly burn took a long time to heal.

When I turned eighteen I took off, hitchhiked to Florida. Working nights as a cocktail waitress let me spend a lot of time on the beach. But I missed Mom, worried about her, and after a few months I hitched back to Atlanta and found myself with a bunch of potheads near Five Points.

Mart Tillian, a guy I'd known in Roswell, showed up a couple of years later. We got high the day I turned twenty-one and got married for the hell of it. Five months later he decided he wanted to go back to Roswell. I got a job in a diner, he hustled drunks for drugs and knocked me around when he came home. We'd been back in Roswell two years when the drunk he hustled wasn't as drunk as Mart thought and signed a complaint. Mart had to stay overnight in lockup before he could make bail. And was stabbed to death before morning.

In spite of the abuse he'd given me I felt guilty but kept going to work, walking around with little interest in anything. Mom came to stay with me. One day while she was still at work Bo came to my apartment and tried to rape me. I told Mom and two weeks later cops were at my door telling me she was dead.

I was terrified Bo would come back, hardly left my apartment, but finally went back to work. Emory walked into the diner and I made the same mistake my Mom had made, married another abuser. I knew that Emory had taken advantage of my mental state after my husband's death and then losing Mom. Did he talk to Mart in jail, learn about me, and was he actually involved in Mart's killing? To what purpose? And where did he get the money he had had when we moved to Wexler Bend?

"But Gloria Tejoso wasn't in Wexler Bend when we moved here, if she'd only been here for a year or so."

I was thinking aloud, but Shac answered. "Maybe something or someone else was here at the time that drew him. And later drew her, too."

"Their biological mother?"

"Maybe."

"But no one's been able to trace her?"

"Not yet. Adoptive family had a picture. We're waiting for it."

Shac walked around the counter to the coffeepot and poured another cup. "We're talking to anyone who might have seen Gloria with someone at the bar. Especially regulars."

"Odd, how Gloria wound up in the same small city as her brother, and maybe her biological mother." Another thought occurred to me. "Or father?"

"We're trying to track down where Emory was living, or crashing, when he came back to town. No hotel or motel clerk admits to recognizing him. Maybe somebody who's seen him will see the newspaper and television spots we're about to run."

"Any likely avenues for finding the identity of the mother?" I asked.

"Military is still checking for either one and some states aren't completely digitized yet so takes a while." He took his mug to the sink. "Got a couple of leads to run down. Keep your door locked." He said the words doggedly, not acknowledging my aggravated sniff.

After he left I took my coffee and sat down at my desk. I was glad the legal pad I'd written my notes on last night still lay facedown. Shac hadn't seen it. Wouldn't have put it past him to pick it up just to snoop but since I was right behind him, he hadn't. Might as well update it. I wrote 'sister to Emory Locke' under Gloria's name and sat staring at it. What we didn't know about the three murder victims, if indeed Emory was a victim, would probably fill a large book. Actually it appeared that what I didn't know about my ex husband would fill at least half of a large book.

Candy's neighbor. I studied the list. Candy Corhn. It was an odd name, sounded sort of fake. Was it? Where had she come from? And how had she wound up in Emory's web of lies. Candy had been found by her neighbor in their apartment. Where had she lived, not a really nice part of town I thought I remembered. I shuffled back through my notes. Yes, 123 Valley Street. One of a couple of streets near an abandoned textile mill. Years ago the original mill owners had built a bunch of houses for its workers. A few derelict businesses and bars on the edges of the area. Hadn't there been a drug raid on that street recently, several dealers arrested. Probably already out on bail.

I Googled the address, found a business listed there. I stared at the screen. Old Town Flowers. Now I remembered seeing a Going Out of Business sign on the building a few months ago while I was on a stakeout in that part of town. Who had bought it if the building had been sold? I went to the county property records website but it still showed the old owner, Flowers, LLC. The transfer of ownership hadn't been posted online, I'd have to go to the Property Tax Records office.

Twenty-Two

I stuffed the pad in my tote bag and headed for the door. And my doorbell rang – again. Damn, my place was beginning to seem like Grand Central Station at rush hour. I flipped the cover on the peephole and saw a surprise visitor. Detective Sergeant Hunter. He must not actually spend a lot of time in Roswell. Unlike Shac he didn't keep punching the bell but stood waiting for me to open the door. Maybe he had more news in addition to what Shac had told me. I set my tote bag on the straight-backed chair and opened the door.

"Well, this is unexpected, Sergeant Hunter. Come in."

"Sorry to barge in on you, Cam. I had some days off available so I thought I'd combine business with pleasure and drive to Tennessee."

He was wearing a light weight jacket over the same or another dark blue striped shirt. He must be partial to stripes. "Coffee? It's still hot, I just turned it off."

"Sure. Thanks." He shrugged off the jacket. I took it and laid it across the back of the sofa.

"We're a little cooler up here in early spring than Georgia. One of the few things I liked about Wexler Bend when Emory first brought me up here."

He followed me to the kitchen and sat on the stool Shac had so recently vacated. Was there some meaning to that? I mentally shook myself. Don't be ridiculous. It's business, he said so.

He shook his head to my offer of sugar or cream and took a sip of the coffee I'd set before him on the counter. "I believe you said Emory never gave you a reason for wanting to move to Wexler Bend, right?"

"Right." Funny. I didn't feel like Hunter was doubting my story as I often did with Shac. Hunter was just clarifying his memory. He didn't have his notebook in front of him.

"But it wasn't just Tennessee? He specifically wanted to come to Wexler Bend?"

"He had the route marked on the map. Told me to pay attention and make sure he didn't miss a turn when we drove up in the rental truck."

He nodded, seemed to encourage me to keep talking. Maybe I should talk to him about it. Hunter was familiar with my life. He'd know where I was coming from. "I was actually afraid even then that Emory would get angry and hit me if I messed up. Even though up to that point he never had. The mountains were new to me. I'd never been out of Georgia except when I hitchhiked to Florida at eighteen, but worried about and missed Mom so went back."

"You had to quit your job. Did he say anything about work here for either of you?"

"No. And we had no money. That I knew about. I didn't know how he got the truck to move us. But I was afraid to ask."

"He didn't mention knowing anyone here?"

I frowned. "When did you talk to Sh – er – Sergeant Lane last?"

My question didn't seem to faze him. "Yesterday about noon. Why?"

"So you don't know about Emory's familial relationship to one of our female victims?"

His surprise seemed genuine. I guessed Shac hadn't called him immediately on learning about the DNA match. And kept it back when he did talk to him. Why? "A DNA match? How are they related?"

"Siblings. Actually, twins."

"No shit? Sorry. Who are the parents?"

"That we don't know yet. The girl was adopted at birth. The mother kept Emory but gave him up, too, when he was about a year old. He was raised in foster care." I looked at him. "You didn't get that information for him?"

He shook his head, face carefully expressionless, I thought. "And neither twin knew about the other?"

"As far as we know. Shac, Sergeant Lane, hasn't found anything to show they ever had any contact here in Wexler Bend."

Hunter had pulled his notebook out now and was scribbling notes in the personal style shorthand every police officer developed. I waited. He stopped writing, staring into space, and seemed to be considering something. Finally he met my eyes. "I brought some information with me. I'll tell you first, because it's from McDonald."

"You went to the prison? Saw my - McDonald?"

"I was owed a favor and managed to wangle my way into a few words with him in solitary. I guess he was tired of it after twenty-nine days and agreed. He met Emory eighteen years ago when they were both in Fulton County jail. Emory was arrested as a juvenile, waiting for transfer to the juvenile facility."

That's probably why he hated my being a security officer, I thought. Even in the private sector. "And?"

"Emory considered himself a real badass, even that young. Then later McDonald ran into Emory in Roswell when he got out of lockup and McDonald was trying to get out of paying a parking ticket. He said Emory bragged that he had an ace in the hole up in Tennessee and was going to come into a lot of money soon."

Another shock. Shac had told me about the connection between Emory and Mart, of course. But Hunter hadn't shared his information about McDonald with Shac. If they were competing, I guess it was a draw. "How?"

"Said Emory didn't tell him. Or could be McDonald didn't want to tell me." He searched my face, an expression I couldn't define in the depths of dark blue eyes. Or maybe I didn't want to define it. "Maybe Emory had money to move because he got an advance from whoever he was expecting to get it from here."

I forced myself to think back to those first months in Wexler Bend. We bought the Wexler Pointe condo and I'd dared to hope a new start would turn my life around. I'd learn to please Emory and he would be a good husband.

105

"He did seem to have plenty of money when we got here. Enough for a good down payment on this condo. Our bills were paid, we had some nice furniture. Then one day he said the money was gone and I had to get a job."

"And that's when you started with Eastern Fabricators?"

I nodded. Then shook my head. "No, for a little over a year I worked at the garden center on the edge of town. But it was seasonal and the hours too variable. Just before my hours would have been cut way back again I heard about a clerical opening at Eastern and applied for it. Emory didn't like it but we needed the money."

"He never came up with a significant amount of money again?"

"Never. He did seasonal work for the garden center, too, had a talent for it. But he never tried for a better job."

Something made an almost audible click in my brain, but when I tried to nail down the connection, it slipped away.

"What happened?" Damn. Hunter was as quick on the uptake as Shac. I really had to work on my poker face.

"I don't know. Something tried to swim to the surface of my mind, but then dived away again."

"Something about Emory?"

"I can't be sure. I think it had to do with him. It'll come back maybe."

He walked over to the window alcove that would have been a dining area except I used it as an office. Narrow fake leaded glass windows flanked sliding glass doors which led to a small enclosed patio. I saw him glance down toward the metal track for the doors and then upward and a faint expression of surprise crossed his face. He'd most likely checked for some kind of rod in the track. There was a rod, but true to my need for redundant security systems, I'd installed a series of small bells attached to the top of the glass doors by nylon fishing line and hanging along the inside of the decorative valance. Any attempt to lift the door from the track would set them jangling and also set off my security alarm.

His next question caught me by surprise. "You've known Sergeant Lane a long time?"

I couldn't keep the sourness from my voice. "Oh, yes. Since the first time a neighbor called the police when Emory was 'teaching me a lesson' as well as destroying the place."

"Sorry. Your encounters with authority haven't been pleasant, have they?"

I shrugged. "I really was grateful for them. For you and Shac."

"I'm glad it didn't turn you against the police. It does some people."

I picked up the coffee carafe and glanced at him. "More coffee?"

"No, I've held you up long enough. You were about to go out, weren't you?" He'd evidently noticed my tote bag in the chair by the door.

After a brief internal debate, I decided to ask if he wanted to see the crime scene where Gloria Tejoso had died.

Twenty-Three

He did want to see the crime scene. He said he'd checked out the mountain and park online. And Shac had sketched in what the police knew up to now. But he'd like to see the actual scene of Gloria's murder. Fern's relief was on duty when we drove up the mountain to the park entrance. I was reminded that I hadn't talked to Fern yet nor asked Shac if the police had gotten any useful information from her. I was doubtful they had, but I'd try to remember to ask.

I pulled off the road at the overlook, which had parking space for half a dozen cars. "You can see the graduated steps of the dam and its base from here. The openings of the spillway channels are about fifteen feet from the top, almost hidden by those small trees and bushes all down the side. The spillways end at a concrete apron on the same level as the base of the dam, with the concrete channel curving on down. Both Gloria and Emory's bodies were visible from here on that apron among fallen rocks."

"How about at the top of the dam? Is there easy access?" He asked.

"Yes. A corner of the lower parking area for the Nature Center is about fifteen yards from the dam. There's a path."

Jake leaned on the stainless steel pipe raised a couple of inches from the top of the concrete wall. "So is there much traffic to and from the park at this time of year?"

"Not as much as in full summer, of course. More when there's a planetarium show."

"And they were killed at night so the killer was apparently not too worried about being seen."

"So it would seem." I replied.

We drove on to the Nature Center parking lot and got out of the car again. Yellow crime scene tape formed an alley toward the low wall at the near end of the dam.

We stepped over it and walked to the dam. Jake leaned over the four foot fence, not as high as the fence that guarded the top of the dam itself, a few feet above us. He stared down through the overhanging tree limbs at the many small and large rocks on the spillway base and on the steps of the dam.

"There are a couple of other places you might be interested to see up here."

He gave me a questioning look. "Crime scenes?"

"Well, one is, though not another murder scene. In the recent past anyway."

"What?"

"You know the roses associated with the murders. I suspect they're from the patch of yellow roses I found up here."

"And the other? And do we ride or walk?" He looked down at his black dress shoes.

"Damn. The blacktop walking trail goes near the second site. It's where Senator Jarvis's wife was 'kidnapped,'" I sketched quote marks with my hands "and left chained to a tree. I'll just tell you about the place where the roses grow."

We walked in silence through the parking lot and found the paved walking trail before he spoke. "I take it you have doubts about the abduction?"

"I do. I believe she might have staged it."

"Okay. What about the roses?" Jake held back a branch that overhung the trail.

"It's an old home site. A big natural rock wall sort of behind it. Nothing still standing of the home except remnants of a low manmade rock edging. And a thicket of yellow rose bushes."

"No connection to the murder cases?"

"As far as I know. I believe it might be the old family home site of Mrs. Jarvis. Her great grandfather gave the land to the city, wanted it named for his wife, Clare Creek Park,

Reservoir and Dam. The reservoir was once the source of water for Wexler Bend, actually."

"C-l-a-r-e? Unusual spelling."

"Her name was really Claire. The creek was named Claire Creek for her, but the early residents called it 'Clare' and it was spelled that way on maps, so it stuck and was accepted as the name."

"All right, playing devil's advocate. If it is her old family home site, wouldn't it cause her to be opposed to the development?"

"I'm not sure. There's something about her. She doesn't seem the sentimental type to dwell on old family ties."

"So she staged the kidnapping. Figuring the development would go through if the opponents were discredited?"

I nodded. I stopped at a spot on the path near a huge oak tree. Smaller trees surrounded it but the area was fairly open and free of undergrowth. From the path to and all around one of the smaller trees the ground was churned up. "I suppose she wanted to be sure she was found." I mused.

"How did you know the place?" Jake asked.

"I've walked over a good portion of this mountain. I recognized it immediately when I saw it on the news."

Jake looked at the rutted earth, smashed down weeds and small bushes. "Rather a lot of trouble. But some folks will go to great lengths for money."

"I bet the paramedics loved it. And the naturalists were wringing their hands."

"Is the home site near here?"

"Half a mile ahead the path curves sharply and the home site is actually almost straight through from here but it's very muddy after a rain. Too far to walk in those shoes."

"Sorry I didn't bring boots." He said with a grin.

"Not much point anyway. Let's remember to ask Shac if he knows whether the roses I received are the same kind as the ones up here."

We both turned and started back. When we reached the parking lot we got in my car and started down the mountain.

After gleaning all she could from the newpaper clipping Gloria read the first letter from Aunt Luisa, addressed to her sister, Teresa. Luisa was a highly paid model in Atlanta. At least that's what she told her mother, Grandma Elena. Grandma pretended to believe her and refused to let any of the family say otherwise in her presence. Luisa came home to visit several times a year, bringing expensive presents. Aunt Luisa had asked Teresa to adopt her friend's baby girl. The whole family knew of Teresa's bitter disappointment that she'd been unable to conceive a child in the five years she'd been married.

Gloria always knew she was adopted. But for her blonde hair, pale complexion and blue eyes in the midst of an expansive, boisterous and loving dark-eyed Hispanic family, she would have suspected Luisa was her birth mother. Teresa loved her only sister, would have done anything for her, so she did adopt her friend's child, named her Gloria, and loved her as her own. And less than a year later Teresa, a maid, had died in the shooting at the Grand Majestic.

The woman in the picture was Caucasian, and Luisa's letter said she was also a high-priced model, or as Gloria now knew, paid escort or call girl. The wealthy, low-level politician who had fathered her child promised to take care of them. But then when the child turned out to be twins, a boy and a girl, he only wanted her to keep the boy. So she had begged Luisa to help her find a good family to take her baby girl. She hoped one day to be reunited with her child, and thought the chances were better if it was a private adoption.

Twenty-Four

I drove out through the park gate and glanced at my dashboard clock. "One o'clock? You must be starving. You had to get up before the crack of dawn to drive up here this morning."

"Actually, I drove straight through from Atlanta after I saw McDonald yesterday afternoon. Traffic on the perimeter was stopped dead for about three hours so I didn't reach the Tennessee line until ten last night. Left a message with my Lieutenant I'd be gone a couple of days."

"Are you staying at the Clare View Hotel?" I hoped he didn't take the question personally. But if he was I could give Zoey a legitimate reason for going back.

Hunter laughed. "Hardly. Out of my reach. I'm at the Red Roof. No restaurant though."

"There's a pretty decent sports bar slash restaurant not far from here. Serves a dark beer from a local microbrewery that a lot of people like. That okay?"

"Sure. Since I'm not officially on duty wouldn't be polite not to try it." He seemed comfortable with me driving us around. I guessed having a female partner for several years had mellowed him toward female drivers, if it had ever bothered him.

We didn't talk much for the ten minutes it took to reach the Rocky Road Sports Bar and Restaurant. The parking lot still had quite a few cars scattered across it. Part of the appeal of the place, along with the food and beer, was the half dozen wall size high definition television screens in the room. If a live game was playing on one near your table, you had to shout to be heard. I hoped ours was near a screen. I didn't want Hunter to bring up the subject of relationships again, because I didn't know what answer to give him.

Two people were walking toward the entrance as we got close to it. I tried for a poker face when I recognized them. Hunter spoke first. "Lane." He stuck out his hand. "I was going to call you after lunch."

Shac's face was a study in surprise until he got it under control and shook Hunter's hand. "Glad to see you, Hunter. Ways from home, aren't you?"

The woman with Shac was eyeing me, not with gladness. I reciprocated.

"Oh, Cam, I don't think you've met Louise. Louise, Cameron Locke and Sergeant Jake Hunter from Georgia."

Hunter shook her hand and I nodded. No way in hell was I going to say I was happy to meet the ex-wife who'd barged into my home to warn me away from her ex-husband. Hunter opened the door and I went in followed by Louise and Shac.

While we waited for the hostess Shac said, "Why don't we sit together? You can tell us some big-city war stories, Hunter."

The expression on Louise's face made it clear she was not in favor of that idea. In which case I was very much in favor of it. Hunter looked at me and I agreed with fake subdued enthusiasm. If Louise Shackleford Taggert's looks were lethal, I'd have been laid out on the floor.

The hostess seated us as far as possible from the nearest big screen. Maybe she thought we wanted to talk. Well, two of us did.

The server took our drink orders. Hunter and I ordered the dark beer. Shac and Louise both ordered sweet tea, saying they had to get back to work after lunch. Hunter told Shac he'd driven up last night after he'd decided to take a few days of the leave he'd accumulated. I thought I saw a look of satisfaction in Louise's eyes as she jumped to the conclusion he was staying with me. Neither Hunter or I disabused her of the idea. On my part, purposely, to keep her off guard. I did not care to speculate on his reason. Nor did I care to speculate on Shac's reaction to the idea, if he reached the same one. What were they doing out to lunch together anyway? Maybe she'd been telling the truth and they were going to reconcile. I ignored the pang that shot through my heart when I admitted the possibility. While we ate Hunter and Shac vied with each other to tell about the most harrowing cases they'd had without going into the gory details.

Louise endured the shop talk through the entrees but finally snapped. "I am certainly glad I'm in corporate law. You two are disgusting. I have to get back to work." She caught herself and smiled sweetly at Shac. "I'll call you later, honey."

She glared at me and left.

"Cam. Are you okay with the shop talk?" Hunter looked contrite.

"Of course, she is." Shac assured him. "She wanted to be a cop herself, didn't you, Cam? She'd have been right in there with the tall tales."

I forced a laugh. Even over a year later my disappointment lingered. I liked being a PI, but I'd really wanted to work up to an official detective's gold shield, too.

Hunter drained his beer and waved the server away when she offered another. "Lane, I've already told Cam. I talked to her stepfather yesterday. Thought maybe he was holding onto some information that might be useful in this case up here. Or even her mother's death."

Shac narrowed his eyes. "And did he? Have any information?"

"Not much. He did tell me he'd run into Emory Locke a couple of times. Once eighteen years go in Fulton County jail when Locke was a juvenile, barely. Then again after he was released from jail in Roswell, where Cam's first husband was killed. They talked and I think Locke made a point of meeting Cam at the diner where she worked."

"McDonald say that?"

"No. It's just my feeling."

"Uh huh."

I could have slapped Shac. He put a lot of store in his own gut feelings about a case.

"I told him about the DNA connection between Gloria and Emory. Who checked that angle for you, Shac?" I asked with great innocence.

He took a swallow of tea. "Hunter was out so when I called it was a Lieutenant Patricia something? She looked it up for me."

"Patrice Consolo." Hunter corrected the name.

"Yeah. Very helpful."

Hunter agreed. "She's as good a superior officer as any. Doesn't make any secret of her agenda, to make sure Hispanic crime victims get as much attention as others." He paused. "Which they should, of course."

"Of course." Shac looked at his watch. He asked, oh, so casually. "You mentioned a case you worked once about a body found at a dam. Have you seen our crime scene at the dam?"

"Actually, yes. Cam took me up there this morning. Long way to fall. If the victims fell. Does your ME say they died from the falls or were they already dead when they went over?"

"ME in Nashville hasn't completed the autopsies yet. Preliminary report, he thinks they were already dead before they went over the dam." Shac snapped his fingers and pulled out his cell phone. "The picture of Gloria's mother finally got here. Her and both babies."

I looked at a faded snapshot of a vibrant young blonde, holding a baby in each arm and flirting with the camera. "Beautiful. Wonder which one is Emory?" Frowning, I pulled the small phone screen closer. "They both inherited her blonde good looks." Again I felt that tug of recognition I'd felt when I saw the picture of Gloria's body. Why? Had I seen her mother's picture, or even her mother, somewhere once?

"That's twice, Cam. You're sure you don't know her?" Shac asked, sharp gaze boring into me.

"No. There's just a feeling I've seen someone like her, or a picture maybe, before."

He replaced his phone in his pocket and pasted a friendly look on his face. We started toward the exit. "So, what are you doing now? Gonna show Hunter the town?"

"I thought we might check out the building where Candy Cohrn was murdered." From the corner of my eye I saw Hunter do a double take.

"What name did you say?"

Shac answered. "Candy Cohrn. She was our first victim. Why?"

"As I left the hotel this morning a report of a missing person out of Miami by that name landed in my cell phone inbox. Blonde, five four or five, slender. Sound like your victim?"

I might have been imagining things, but I thought I saw an expression of relief cross Shac's face when Hunter said 'the hotel.' He had a lot of nerve being relieved that I wasn't having a fling with Sergeant Hunter when he'd been having lunch with his ex-wife.

"Damn." He pulled out his phone again and paged through his own notifications. When he found it, he held the phone so we could see. Hunter and I both nodded.

Shac was reading the information about the missing girl. "Guess I better let them know we found their missing person." He headed for his car. Before he got there he turned. "Hey, Hunter, feel free to hang out with me or at the station while you're here."

Hunter laughed and waved. "Thanks. I'll stick with Cam today, since she's the one what brought me." Shac continued to his car and got in.

"Still want to look at the other crime scene?" I asked.

He agreed. "Neighbor found her, right? Are you familiar with the area?"

"Yes, I had a – " I broke off. Did Hunter really know I was a private investigator? Might as well find out. We were on my turf now. "Are you aware that I'm a PI now?"

He grinned. "Of course. Even know your license number."

I grinned back. "That background check when I was in Roswell, huh?"

"Like being a PI?" "Yes. I do. Set my own hours, pick my cases, unlike you police gumshoes."

"But you'd still prefer being a police gumshoe?"

I sighed. "That ship has sailed. I had to get over it."

He had the good sense to leave that statement alone. Neither of us said anything else until we were back in town. When a traffic light caught me Jake shifted in his seat and spoke in an offhand way. "She girlfriend or wife?"

I didn't look at him. Or pretend I didn't know who he meant. "Louise? Ex-wife."

"Seems to be having thoughts of reverting to non-ex."

I shrugged. "Maybe."

"And seems to consider you something of a rival."

I really didn't want to discuss Shac's relationship, or not, with his former wife so my answers were a little short. "She's wrong."

Jake either didn't or didn't want to catch the hint. "Neither remarried?"

"She did."

Twenty-Five

I could almost hear his next question but before he could voice it, I turned onto Valley Street. It looked even drabber and less inviting than I remembered. "Here's the area where Candy lived. And died."

"Before you started to say – what? You had a case in the area?"

"Stakeout. Noticed the building nearby, flower shop going out of business."

Garbage spilled out of several of the cans lined up along the street. I parked two doors up from the shop between an ancient Buick with side panels so rusty they were lacy-looking and a newer Chevrolet. Crime scene tape still stretched across the front of the two story building that had housed the flower shop. Since it was taller than its neighbors on either side two windows on the upper floor of the building were in our line of sight. Dark curtains flapped from a broken pane in one of the windows. I sketched the details of the finding of the girls body. I realized he probably didn't know about Emory's connection to Candy either and told him. We discussed the possibility that she came to Wexler Bend with Emory in the first place, since both came from Florida.

I was about to suggest that he might want me to drop him off at the police station when I saw a familiar nondescript faded blue Kia pull up in front of the building. Shac saw us and waved in a 'come here' motion. I looked at Hunter and he nodded. We got out of the car and went to meet Shac.

He had a key ring in his hand and led us toward the empty flower shop as he talked. "I figured Cam wanted to see this crime scene close-up and thought you might be interested, too, Hunter."

I thought of something I'd meant to ask Shac. "The neighbor who found her. Did she say if Candy lived alone? In this seedy part of town?"

"He. And he didn't know, only moved in himself a month ago. Said he never saw anybody else in the place, but he's a junkie. Gone now." He went to a door on the left side of the front of the building. I could see steep stairs through the glass pane, which had a crack almost its entire length. No wonder Candy worked the morning shift. Who'd want to come home at night to this drug infested neighborhood and fumble to get in the door.

Shac found the right key. The ancient lock resisted at first, but he kept working it and it finally clicked. He went through first motioning us to hang back. He disappeared at the top of the stairs and then reappeared, saying, "Okay. Come on up."

When we reached the top of the stairs, I saw there were two doorways on the right wall of the landing. More crime scene tape about four feet up from the floor had been stretched across the one nearer the front. It had either fallen down or Shac had pulled it loose on one side and let it drop. The door stood open. We entered and looked around the tiny living room. Shac didn't caution us not to touch anything since the scene had already been processed. But even though I'm a tactile person, I had no desire to touch anyway. The furnishings, such as they were, included a sagging floral print couch, mismatched chair with its cushion on the floor, a small TV on a stand and a couple of rickety tables with tattered magazines stacked on them. A bare low-wattage bulb dangled from the ceiling.

I walked into the even tinier kitchen. No table or chairs. Black trash bag on the floor overflowing with paper plates and plastic takeout containers. The tiniest microwave oven I'd ever seen sat on a low cabinet between the apartment size sink and a two burner stove. The only upper cabinets were over the sink. A two cup sauce pan sat on one of the stove burners, its bottom covered by some unidentifiable black substance. The cabinet doors stood open revealing a couple of boxes of frosted corn flake cereal, a jar of peanut butter, half a dozen or so ready to heat prepared dinners, all neatly arranged by height. No cans, probably because no can opener was in evidence.

I walked over to the only new looking item in the room, a shiny black dorm refrigerator. Using one finger I opened it. Two quart milk containers, mustard and ketchup, orange juice and a jar of black olives, all also arranged by height. I could feel Shac looking at me from the opening to the living room. I brushed past him and went through the living room to the bedroom.

Stripped bed, dark stain on the mattress. The heavy ceramic angel no doubt rested in the evidence room at police headquarters. Besides the bed the only furniture was another rickety table and a nicked and scratched little dresser with a cloudy mirror. On the table was a cheap alarm clock and small lamp with a torn shade. On the dresser toiletries were neatly lined up by height. A can of hair spray, brush, nail polish, liquid makeup, cheap cologne, all from a dollar store.

"Dollar store razor, shampoo and conditioner in the bathroom?" I looked at Shac.

"Two razors. And shaving crème."

"He was here." I said in a flat voice.

"For the record, are you saying Emory Locke lived here with the victim. Why do you think that?"

"The same reason you thought so. His OCD. Everything had to be arranged by height."

He nodded, made a notation in his notebook. "Anything else either of you want to see?"

"No. Let's get out of here."

Out on the street again Hunter allowed that, yes, he'd like to check out the Wexler Bend police department. So I parted company with them and left alone.

Twenty-Six

I took a roundabout way home which took me past Wexler Bend Hospital. A small crowd spilled out from the roundabout that curved in front of the entrance. I slowed and lowered my car window. The car in front stopped to let an older couple cross the street. I asked the nearest person, a heavy set woman with a dark red curly perm, "What's happened?"

She was happy to pass on what she knew or thought she knew. Her small light eyes glittered. "Senator Jarvis was brought in by ambulance half an hour ago. There's a rumor he was shot."

"Who's supposed to have shot him?"

"His wife. Can you believe that? And he took her back after she left him, telling all them stories about him."

The car ahead of me moved on and so did I. "Thanks." I called back to my informant.

I debated parking and going inside. But the chance of seeing Jarvis was slim to none, if he was indeed shot. If he was, and Rhoda Jarvis did the shooting, why had she done it? I probably wouldn't get a chance to talk to Tabi either with a prominent person being on the premises. Hopefully I'd see her tonight at our Eastern Fabricators ex-employees informal get-together. So I bit the bullet and called Shac's cell phone.

He answered after one ring. "Yeah, Cam. You heard?"

"I was driving by the hospital and saw the crowd. A woman said Jarvis had been shot. Is it true?"

"No, fell down the stairs according to his wife. We're doubling back to the hospital now." Not to my surprise, he added. "And no, you can't be there."

I drove on to my condo. If Shac dropped Hunter off back at my place he'd tell me what there was to know.

Maybe I'd take him to the dinner with my former colleagues from Eastern. I thought about Candy Cohrn as I drove. When I reached home I booted up my computer. Maybe the real estate company who had listed the property briefly knew why Candy decided to come back home. For lack of any better idea I did a search for 'flower shops, Wexler Bend, Tennessee.'

The first link was to a story in the Wexler Chronicle last year. The article said that Old Town Flowers was one of the oldest family-owned businesses in town. But the owner, Summer Cohrn, sixty-seven years old, had suffered a serious heart attack and was not expected to recover and continue to operate the shop. Authorities were attempting to locate her estranged daughter, Candace. "Candy" Cohrn. Not a fake name after all. Shades of the sixties.

A link a little further down the page was to Summer Cohrn's obituary last October. And another to a listing of the property with Wesale Realty. But there had been no realty sign on the shop today when Shac, Jake and I were there. Evidently Candy had changed her mind about selling the property and returned to Wexler Bend to live above the shop. With Emory. I would be willing to bet that returning to Wexler Bend was his idea, though his motive was still a mystery to me.

I looked up the real estate company, got the telephone number and checked the time. The office should still be open.

Their phone was picked up on the second ring. "Wesale Realty, this is Pansy. Which of our property listings interests you?"

"I'm interested in a storefront property on Valley Street. You did have it listed. Have you sold it?"

. "I'm sorry. That listing was withdrawn by the owner. But we have many other excellent downtown properties we could show you."

I tried for real regret in my voice. "Oh, I did want that one. An older building. Why did the owner withdraw it? Is the flower shop going to reopen?"

"I couldn't say, ma'am. The owner had been living out of town and decided to return. But we have a couple of other older buildings listed."

"Let's see. An odd name, Com – no – Corhn, that was the name of the flower shop owner, wasn't it? I didn't realize she'd moved away."

"No, ma'am. Mrs. Cohrn passed away last year. Her daughter inherited the building and came back, but unfortunately, she also passed away. I probably shouldn't say this, but the young lady was – " she paused, probably looking around furtively to make sure no one could hear her " – she was murdered so it may be a while before the building is available again." "I guess she decided to come home after her mother died. Too late. So many people do that. Do you think that's what she did? Did she have any other relatives here in town who might inherit? Maybe I could talk to them."

"None that we know of, ma'am. Please come on into the office and I'm sure we can find something to suit you."

I supposed Candy hadn't given the realty company any reason for deciding to keep the building and come home. If returning to Wexler Bend was Emory's idea, he would have made sure Candy only said what he wanted her to say, to anyone, just as he had me for so long.

"Thank you. Goodbye." Did I remember to block my caller ID before I dialed the number? Lord, I hoped so. Shac would be sure to find out and say I was interfering with his investigation.

While I sat mulling over what I'd learned, my cell phone pinged for an incoming text message. Shac. His usual terse message. 'flower shop owned by Candy. Real name.' The ring for an incoming call pushed the text message off the screen before I could respond. Jake Hunter. When I answered he told me the same thing. So Shac was now keeping him informed, too. I decided not to tell either that I had already found that information myself. He said he'd see me soon and hung up.

It hadn't taken long for Gloria to find the list of shooting victims at the Grand Majestic when she visited the Journal-Constitution morgue archive. The paper had published it along with pictures the day after the shooting massacre. No one had ever been charged although several low level thugs had been questioned. Only one of the three party women was a pale blonde. The paper listed them before the two maids, one of which, of course, was Gloria's adopted mother, Teresa. The blonde was the same one in the two pictures Gloria had laid on the desk beside the computer screen.

A follow up story two days after the shooting named the blonde, Daisy Montague, and the two others, a redhead and a brunette – Aunt Luisa? - as being regulars on the Atlanta party circuit. The accompanying picture showed Daisy on the arm of a tall, handsome man with a wide smile, showing all his teeth. The man was identified as an up and coming politician from Tennessee, Wiley Jarvis. Was Wiley Jarvis her biological father? If so, did he know about the twins he fathered? Was he still in politics in Tennessee?

She grabbed her pictures and notes, thanked the attendant and hurried home. Sitting down at her desk she opened her laptop computer and launched an Internet search for Wiley Jarvis. Wiley Jarvis was indeed still in politics. At least on the state level. Evidently he had never advanced to national office, but had been a senator in the state legislature from the Eastern part of the state for the last fifteen years. Married to Rhoda Jarvis nee Shell, a prominent family in that end of the state. No mention of children.

When she clicked the next link on the search results page it brought up the picture of her mother on Jarvis's arm, the same picture the Atlanta paper had run. The picture had been shot in Nashville, according to the cut below it. It was an old tabloid story published soon after Jarvis married Rhoda Shell. The story below the picture speculated on any expectations Daisy might have had of becoming Mrs. Jarvis herself prior to the senator's marriage. Had the young Daisy had such expectations? Especially after the birth of her twins? And had the party-going politician led her to expect it?

Twenty-Seven

Shac dropped Hunter off at my place at five. I'd showered, dressed and applied minimal makeup by the time he rang the bell.

He stepped back when he saw what I was wearing, dark creased slacks and pale blue sweater set. "Uh oh, this was a bad idea. I didn't know you had a date."

I pulled a face. "Hardly. Though my dinner companions will probably think you're my date, if I can talk you into going with me."

"I thought you'd never ask. Where are we going? And you'll need to run me to my hotel so I can shower and change."

"No problem. And it's an informal get-together of former Eastern Fabricators employees. We meet every three months or so at the Rocky Road, if you don't mind twice in one day."

"Will the ex-Mrs. Shac be there?" He threw up an arm in mock defense. "Sorry, couldn't resist. She didn't need ice in her tea. I'm surprised the glass didn't freeze solid."

"Uptown lawyer hang out with losers? Hardly. She was in Legal. After the plant closed she married an Eastern VP, went into private practice then left town." I grabbed my tote. "You can tell me what you all found out at the hospital on the way."

"I knew you had an ulterior motive. Will your former co-workers object? To my being there?"

"No. Our numbers have dwindled in a year. A few moved out of town for work, a few others have jobs and can't get off."

"Okay, give." I said after we were buckled in and on our way to the Red Roof, just a few miles away and on the way to the Rocky Road.

"Not much to give. The senator lost his grip on the banister and tumbled down the main staircase in his home, according to his wife. The senator told the same story." "I hear a 'but,'" I said.

"He won't allow her in his hospital suite."

"Won't allow Rhoda in his suite? Or she won't go?"

Hunter looked over toward me. "Why do you say that?"

"I met her once. In a women's shelter. And you can forget I said that. You know how secretive they have to be. Did Jarvis give a reason for not wanting her in the room?"

"Not to us. If he told his doc, he's not sharing."

I drove awhile in silence, thinking about it. Now that I thought about it, Jarvis had never given a statement to the press about his wife's being chained to a tree on Clare Creek Mountain. Not for their lack of trying to get a statement. Strange.

I pulled through the Red Roof parking lot and up under the entrance overhang. "Grab your shower and I'll pick you up in half an hour. Got an errand to run."

"I'll be waiting. Thanks."

I'd caught a glimpse of a familiar nondescript vehicle pull into a space as I drove through the parking lot. I circled the hotel as though I was leaving through the back exit. But I parked near the service entrance and walked around the building. Keeping cars between us I quietly approached Daniel Traynor's favorite surveillance vehicle on the drivers' side. I passed my hand near the hood. Felt heat, so I hadn't been mistaken. His head was down, as he fiddled with a parabolic mike focused on the hotel entrance through the passenger window.

"Domestic job?" I asked.

He whirled toward me. "Damn, Cam. Scared the piss out of me. I taught you too well."

I went around, opened the passenger side door and got in. "I'd think you'd be over at the hospital instead of here."

He didn't say anything for a minute, just stared at me. "Why would you think that?"

"Well, your client is presently a patient there. After a fall, it seems."

"My client." He was silent for another minute. "I guess you saw the invoice I was working on when you came to my office the other day."

"That would be a yes. Just the name, though, before the screensaver came on."

"And you know I have the screensaver password protected. Or you would have checked it out."

"Hey, you could have gotten careless. But I didn't try, didn't want any other goodies your computer might have ratting me out."

"You never know, do you?" He remarked.

"I didn't know you'd gone over to the dark side. Working for Senator Jarvis? Please."

"His money's as good as any." He saw my expression. "Well, if it's dirty money it's never been proved."

I let it go. "How long have you been on this gig?"

"Couple of days."

"You didn't say but you must be on a domestic spying mission. People in the Senator's circle don't stay at the Red Roof."

He still didn't confirm or deny. But he'd said a couple of days. Hunter had been here for a couple of days. And Daniel had arrived just now as I pulled up to let Hunter out. I didn't want to even entertain where this line of thought was going. My old mentor tailing me? Because I was with a detective from Roswell, Georgia? The town where two recent murder victims in Wexler Bend, one of them my ex husband, had been born? Why was my mind connecting Daniel's stake out at the Red Roof with Sergeant Jake Hunter?

I checked my watch. "Gotta pick up my date. Save you some effort, we'll be at the Rocky Road with my usual crowd from Eastern. Back corner table."

The expression on his face was almost enough to mollify me for his tailing me and not telling me why. Almost.

Twenty-Eight

Thirty minutes later I was introducing Hunter to a half-dozen former co-workers, three of their wives and two husbands. "Tabi not here yet? And Zoey said she'd be here tonight."

Just as I asked, Tabi, my source at the hospital, and Zoey came in and headed for our table. When Zoey saw me her usual happy smile dimmed a little. She was still peeved about my behavior at the conference center, I guessed. They found seats and I introduced Hunter to them. Everyone ordered drinks.

Carl, a big guy, CNA, who'd assisted Tabi in Eastern's medical department and now worked as an EMT, turned toward her. "So what's the scoop on Senator What's-In-It-For-Me, Tab? His wife finally shoot him or not?"

"Carl, you know I can't discuss hospital patients. I will say this, he was not shot. And that's it."

Just then our server returned with the tray of drinks. After she'd taken our food orders Carl pointed his beer bottle at the nearest big screen. Everyone turned to see what had caught his attention. The wide black ribbon for a breaking news story was running across the bottom. The football game above was muted, and the usual staccato musical intro hadn't been audible above the conversation noise level in the room. As we all faced the screen someone turned up the volume and I caught the words '...rushed to the hospital this afternoon by ambulance. According to his aide the Senator fell down some stairs in his home and injured his arm.' The story crawled across the screen once more and ended.

Several people looked at Carl. "Weren't you on the call, Carl?"

"No, we were across town trying to keep a juvenile diabetic from lapsing into a coma."

"Guess Tabi was telling us the truth, Carl." Susan, who'd worked in production, said. "The question is, did he fall, or was he pushed?"

Tabi just shrugged and turned up her bottle of dark beer. She loved the stuff. Maybe too much, I sometimes thought. But she was my friend. She'd treated my breaks, bruises and sprains at Eastern, finally getting through to me about doing something about it.

The conversation moved on to the efforts of some of our number who still had not found other jobs. Their unemployment insurance was close to ending and Ned Walker, who had five kids, was getting desperate, he said. "At this point I'd take almost anything. Anybody got somebody they want knocked off?"

I knew he was joking but with the recent murders in Wexler Bend, his offer fell a little flat.

Zoey said. "That isn't really funny, you know, Ned. Two of the recent murder victims worked where I do."

"God, I'm sorry, Zoey. You know I didn't mean it."

"I know. Just don't say things like that. Somebody might think you did." Zoey replied.

"Be right back." Tabi excused herself and left the table, heading toward the ladies room. No wonder. I hadn't consciously counted, but I thought she'd downed four beers in fairly quick succession.

"Me, too." I slid my chair back and followed her. I caught the door as it swung closed behind her. She glanced back, gave a small rueful smile, said, "You, too?." She disappeared into a stall.

I stepped into a stall, too, but made sure to exit before she did. While we stood at the sink, she glanced over, not smiling. I could see by the glaze in her pretty hazel eyes that she had a little buzz on, but she said, "I'm not going to tell you anything, either, Cam. We're friends, but I can't tell tales about patients. You know that."

"I know. But you can verify something I already know. That the Senator won't allow his wife into his suite."

The eyes cleared a little with surprise. "There's always somebody." She muttered, more to herself than me.

"Did he visit her when she was taken to the hospital after being found on the mountain?" I asked almost as an afterthought.

Tabi seemed to be thinking of something else when she answered in the same low voice. "No, he was taking a chemo... " She caught herself. "You need to forget I said that, Cam. I can't lose my job. I'm the only one my sister has to depend on."

"Don't worry. I'd never do anything to jeopardize your job." I hugged her and we left the restroom.

I found it difficult to fully participate in the conversation at the table after my brief talk with Tabi in the ladies room. I caught Jake looking at me with a speculative expression a couple of times. Tabi took her leave soon after we returned, citing an early shift next morning. When a few others left also, I told Jake I was ready to go. As we left I noticed almost everyone in the party paying their bill and throwing tips on the table.

When we were in my car and on the way back to the Red Roof, he said, "Okay, your turn. Give."

"Give what?" I tried to manufacture an innocent tone.

"What did you find out in the ladies room from your friend?"

"She gave me the same song and dance, which is true, and she can't afford to lose her job. She cares for a disabled sister."

He wasn't buying it. "That may be so. But she must have let something slip. You were hardly in the room after you came back to the table."

"I promised I'd protect her. She really needs her job."

"Did it have anything to do with the fact he won't allow his wife into his suite?"

I glanced at him. "I already knew that. You told me. But there's something you didn't tell me." He had the grace to look away. "I promised Shac." And in a blatant attempt to move to another subject. "I couldn't break my word to him and make a play for the woman he's smitten with, too."

And it worked. "Of all the bullshit. He was with his ex-wife at lunch, if you recall." I heard myself answer, in a way louder voice than I meant to use. Then the other part of his sentence hit me. "If that's what you're doing, forget it. I'm through with relationships. My track record leaves a hell of a lot to be desired."

"People change. You have. In a way very few women do." There was a serious note in his voice that I ignored. No way was I going there. Even if his eyes reminded me of a dark blue sapphire with mysterious depths that might mean something. Or not.

The thought goaded me to go back to the previous subject. "What else do you know that you haven't told me? Why was Senator Jarvis going thr..." I bit off the word.

"Hmmm." I felt him look at me. "He told his security people to get her off of the estate and not let her back in."

"What?" I almost drove past the hotel and jerked the wheel over at the last minute.

"She wasn't too happy about it either. Tried to get an injunction to get back in. But the judge sided with the Senator. Hardly surprising."

He waited a few seconds, then answered the question I hadn't finished. "Your state senator is quite ill. Terminally ill. And weak. So I guess we can count him out as the killer."

Twenty-Nine

I was trying to take in both his statements and stopped short of the entrance. Seeing it reminded me that I hadn't checked to see if Daniel had followed us to the Rocky Road and back here. I looked in the rear view mirror and all around as I pulled on up under the overhang.

Hunter seemed to read my mind. "He didn't follow us. But I think I saw him pass the restaurant as we got out of the car. Friend of yours? You told him where we were going?"

"Damn." I looked at him as he opened the door. "Does anything get past you and Shac?"

He gave a mock salute. "Exalted company. That's why we're called detectives, remember?" He closed the car door and walked toward the double glass doors of the hotel.

Driving to my condo, I couldn't shake the feeling that had gripped me when I heard about Jarvis's illness. I was sure it had something to do with the murders. But what could it possibly be? And what was my ex-husband's and his twin's, connection with the murders? Aside from being victims, of course. But why were they victims? What had brought them both to Wexler Bend and was it the reason they lost their lives here? Emory had presumably brought Candy Cohrn to Wexler Bend. Why? And why was she killed? Had she known why Emory had returned and the killer didn't want that known?

The feeling that I knew something I hadn't connected to the case tickled the back of my mind again. But I still couldn't identify it. I had a feeling that Emory hadn't come back solely because of me. He'd evidently not wanted me to know he was back in town or he would have made sure I did know. Another question. Why not? If he'd been the one to leave roses for Gloria, Candy and me, one would think he wanted to kill me. But instead he'd been his old arrogant self, telling me I'd be begging him to take me back before long. And now he was dead. When I got home I changed into my threadbare polka dot pajamas. Then sat and leaned back in my office chair and tried to let my mind float freely. Yellow roses found near all the murder victims. Yellow roses on Clare Creek Mountain. On bushes that had been planted long ago. Why those roses? Somebody watching me when I first found the roses, and later when I went back to look at them. Not a spirit, but an actual person. The park was a public area, anybody had access. Even if they paid admission and came through the gate, visitors' names were not logged. And if any shy, or cheap, visitor was in shape to climb the steep side of the mountain to avoid the admission fee, the park was not fenced except for the wolf enclosure. I could mention my sense that I was being watched to Shac and he could check Fern's visitor log, but it was probably futile.

Gloria Tejoso and Emory killed and thrown over the dam that held back Clare Creek Reservoir on the mountain. Candy Cohrn, Emory's girlfriend from Florida, killed in her apartment. All by the same person? Yellow roses left on the front porch of Emory's ex-wife, me. By the killer? Again, why?

State Senator Jarvis's abused and estranged, once and now again, wife kidnapped and left bound to a tree on the mountain. But not killed. Was it really the work of members of the Mountain Marsh Militia to try and force the senator to abandon the development project? Possible but I had my doubts. None of the people I'd seen at the rally seemed the type. Shac had never told me anything he might have learned from the female I'd tagged as an undercover cop who was present.

The only person involved in this case that I'd ever met was Emory. I'd seen Gloria at the rally and the undercover cop, I was sure she was a cop, but didn't know either one. And how did Gloria become involved in the MMM? She'd been in Wexler Bend less than a year according to her employment record at the bar, Shac said. No record in Georgia that she'd ever been a tree hugger or even shown any interest in environmental issues. And speaking of back in town, I still didn't know why Emory had been back in Wexler Bend. He'd laughed off the question. Of course, I'm sure he didn't want me to know he was living in a tiny squalid apartment over a closed flower shop with a lovely young woman years younger than him. Had Candy been Emory's ticket back to Wexler Bend? Again, for what purpose? If he'd thought he might gain back some control and put me under his thumb again, why hadn't he made any move to let me know he was back? I'd only found it out by chance when I saw him on the Jarvis estate. Why had he been there? As a former constituent? What could he have wanted from the state senator suspected of taking bribes?

Returning home. Rhoda Jarvis had left and then returned to the home she shared with an abusive husband. As I recalled, she'd stayed a couple of weeks at the women's shelter. She'd been insistent that I shouldn't remain with my own abusive husband. Why? If rumor could be believed, Jarvis had not only been abusive, he'd cheated on his socialite wife almost from the beginning of the marriage. Although Jarvis seemed to have plenty of money, through questionable means some thought, he needed more respectability. I could see why he'd married into Rhoda's family and social standing which gave him stature in the community to aid his political ambitions.

But why did she marry him? Hadn't I read that at one time her great grandparents had owned almost all of Clare Creek Mountain? They deeded the park acreage to the city of Wexler Bend, which also included their family homestead. Their only son, Rhoda's grandfather, had built a lavish home nearer town overlooking the river and had no interest in living on the mountain. Rhoda's father, an only son, divorced, died in a hunting accident when she was ten years old. She'd grown up in the riverside estate living with her grandparents. Even more elaborately enlarged now, it was home to Rhoda Shell Jarvis and her husband, State Senator Wiley Jarvis.

My God. Could the old home site on the mountain where I'd discovered the yellow rose thicket still growing and thriving be the old Shell family home? Rhoda Jarvis was left bound to a tree near that area. Who had kidnapped her? Or had she actually been kidnapped? For the sake of argument was Rhoda upset about the possible development in the park, that it might destroy her old family homestead? Did she think that if someone kidnapped his wife her husband would stop the development? Hard to believe she would have thought that after all his abuse.

I had to talk to Rhoda Jarvis. If she knew anything about the killings, or knew if her husband was involved, I'd get it out of her. So how did I locate her? If she was not allowed on the Jarvis estate, where might she be staying? The answer was obvious when I thought about it. Clare View Hotel. As I'd told Daniel last night people like Jarvis didn't stay at the Red Roof Motel. There was just one problem. How did I find out her room number and get in to see her? Well, I'd ferreted out information better hidden than a hotel room number. I could do it.

Wexler Bend was even smaller than Gloria had expected. Having lived all her life in the largest city in the Southern United States she wondered if she could manage this. She had to if she was going to find any information about, she was sure he was, her biological father. She hoisted her suitcase into the bus station locker and spun the lock.

To arrive by air, she would have had to fly into Charlotte or Memphis, then to Knoxville and take a puddle jumper, which she could not tolerate, to Wexler Bend.

Outside the sun was shining from a bright blue sky. A cool breeze tossed her blonde hair lightly. She waited until the Charlotte bound Greyhound idling in the nearest bus space had pulled out, then dialed Wesale Realty.

"Wesale Realty, Pansy. Which of our great properties can we show you today?" A chirpy young female voice answered on the third ring.

"Gloria Tejoso. I called you from Atlanta and have just arrived in town by bus. Do you have some furnished apartments to show me?"

"By bus. Oh, yes, Ms. Tejoso." The receptionist's voice had lost a bit of its enthusiasm. "Let me send you to Ms. Leiner. One moment, please."

Several minutes passed before another voice came on the line. "Ms. Tejoso, we do have several furnished units in the price range you gave us." Ms. Leiner told her. "One is in an exclusive condo complex. But perhaps you'd like something a little more economical?"

Thinks I'm a deadbeat because I traveled by bus, Gloria thought. "No. Let's look at that one first. I'm renting a car, I'll be at your office in half an hour or so."

"Ah, yes, all right."

A big smile brightened Ms. Leiner's long face when Gloria pulled up in front of Wesale Realty. Gloria figured the late model Mazda she'd rented when an Audi was not available had something to do with the agent's attitude. Leiner leaned down to the lowered window and asked if Gloria wanted to follow her to the condo. Gloria saw the agent eyeing her Vanderbilt business suit, somewhat wrinkled from the long bus trip, and the Coach bag on the passenger seat. I could have shoplifted both, but what does she care.

She'd debated what to wear on the bus. And opted for the Vanderbilt because she'd rather thought she might run into Ms. Leiner's type when she reached Wexler Bend. She didn't want to be shown run-down apartments in the wrong part of town. When she contacted Senator Jarvis she wanted him to know it had been his loss to abandon his children.

The condo Leiner showed her was in Wexler Pointe Homes, spacious and nicely furnished. She took it immediately and wrote Wesale Realty a check for the hefty deposit and first and last months' rent. After Gloria's name was safely on the six-month lease agreement and her check in hand, Leiner indulged in a little gossip.

She said most of the condos were owned and occupied by successful business people but a few were a little questionable. A private investigator lived in a unit two streets over. The couple had bought their unit when the development was new and the wife stayed home for a while, then became an executive at a now closed plant. Neighbors had called police several times about domestic disturbances at the home before the husband left. Gloria made note of the name. She might need the services of another private investigator since the first one she'd tried hadn't worked out.

The realty agent finally drove away and Gloria carried her luggage inside to the bedroom. Leaving unpacking for later she set her laptop and tablet on the bedside table and plugged in their power supply cables to charge them.

While they charged she drove around the condo complex to get the lay of the land, making note of the street where the private detective lived. Returning to her own unit she parked in her driveway and went inside, activating the security code the realty agent had given her. She pulled a map of Wexler Bend and a stack of printouts from her tote bag and went over them again. She had found the address of the Senators estate online and was happy to see that it was not that far away from the complex.

She looked at her watch, four o'clock. Someone might still be in Senator Jarvis's office. She dialed the number and it rang six times before an answering service picked up and invited her to leave a message. She thought not and hung up. She'd try again in the morning.

A long hot shower and then find a restaurant for dinner. Or she could find a grocery store, get take out and buy some breakfast stuff, especially coffee. A new looking Gevalia machine along with an espresso machine stood on the kitchen counter.

Thirty

I checked the time. A few minutes after ten. Rhoda Jarvis had liked to stay up and watch the late night talk shows at the shelter. She'd still be up. I should have kept on the clothes I'd worn to dinner. They still lay across the bed so I changed into them. Zoey was off duty, but I was sure she'd left instructions to all the staff to watch out for me and keep me from going anywhere near Rhoda Jarvis. Shac probably knew her room number, but he'd raise holy hell if I asked him for it. I couldn't wake up Tabi and she probably wouldn't know anyway.

My only option was to fall back on one of the throw away cell phones I kept on hand for just such occasions. I unlocked the desk drawer and dug one out. I generally kept them charged. I hoped I had. I turned it on and decided to be Helen Keys, her social secretary. I happened to know Helen's husband was in a rehab center, recovering from a fractured hip. Please, God, let Keys be with her husband and not Rhoda right now.

The desk clerk at the hotel answered. "Clare View Hotel. This is Carl, how may I direct your call?"

"Housekeeping, please."

"One moment, please."

After thirty seconds another phone was picked up. "Housekeeping. Lola."

I went into full inept girly mode. "Lola, thank God you're on duty. This is Helen Keys, social secretary to Mrs. Rhoda Jarvis. I was there this afternoon and registered for her." I was guessing, hoped I was right. "I'm sure I wrote her room number in my day planner, but I'm at my husband's rehab center and the planner's at home. Please tell me the number."

"I can transfer your call. Carl should have, Ms…"

I cut her off quickly, "Oh, please, no. She'll be so upset with me. She might fire me. I can't afford to lose my job." I crossed my fingers. "My husband being in the hospital, too." "We're not supposed to give out a guest's room number, Ms. Keys."

"I know. And I promise you won't get into trouble. She'll never know I had to get it from you." I devoutly hoped.

"All right. She's in the VIP suite on the sixth floor. I believe room service has just retrieved her dinner tray."

"Thank you, so much, Lola. You just saved my life. You're a jewel." Careful, don't spread it too thick, I told myself. I made a note that only I could interpret in a notepad to remind myself who I had called this time with the phone and put it back in the drawer along with the phone.

I set the alarm and just as the door clicked shut behind me my house phone rang. I hoped it wasn't Shac. He'd keep digging tomorrow to find out where I'd gone. On the other hand he knows I'm a PI, which necessitates being out at all hours. I'd just let him think that. I was determined that I would not be thwarted in my effort to talk to Rhoda Jarvis this time.

My dash clock still showed a few minutes before eleven o'clock when I parked at the hotel. I knew where the stairs farthest from and out of the desk clerk's line of sight were located. I tried to give every impression that I was just a guest who didn't want to wait for the elevator as I pulled the stair door open. Six flights. Oh well, nothing ventured, nothing gained.

On the sixth floor outside the VIP suite door, I paused to catch my breath for as many minutes as I dared, then knocked.

"Yes, who is it?" Rhoda called in the sharp voice she used to speak to those she considered beneath her notice.

"Ah.. room, ah..mumble, mumble."

"My tray's already... Oh, just a minute." I heard footsteps approach the door and it swung open. Almost as soon as it was open, she started to close it. I stuck my foot in the crack.

She struggled for just a second then abandoned the attempt to close me out. "I'm calling hotel security. This is harassment."

"You might want to wait on that. Do the news outlets know your husband won't allow you in your own home?"

She stopped and whirled around. "You don't know what you're talking about. Are you threatening me, Locke?"

"Certainly not." I stepped into the room and closed the door. The living room of the suite was lavish, even had a fireplace with a cozy seating arrangement of sofa and chairs arranged in front of it. She stood near the long sofa table. A fat glass lamp with pleated shade stood on the table, along with several heavy-looking statuettes and a translucent gold candy dish.

"But if you call security the media will find out and will want to know why you're here rather than at your home."

"You're mistaken. I'm here because it's closer to the hospital."

"He won't allow you in his hospital room either." I leaned against the door. "Why not?

"My husband was injured. He needs rest."

"Did he visit you when he put you in the hospital?" I watched her closely.

She drew herself up to her full five feet ten inches. "I have always been a little accident prone."

"Yeah. That's what I used to tell people."

"Well, you probably should choose husbands more carefully, my dear." Sarcasm was heavy in her voice.

"You told me I should leave and not look back. Why didn't you? You went back to your husband after he beat the crap out of you."

"What? That he beat you or that you went back?"

"I ordered you to leave my room."

"Was your husband involved in the murders of those young women?"

She sucked in a breath, looked down. "Of course not. Don't be ridiculous." I noticed a sidelong look toward me as she turned away. To see if I believed her?

"My husband is a respected Tennessee legislator. How could you think he could be involved in the deaths of those girls?" The woman was protesting way too much. What was her game?

"Respected, right. For the last two years he's worked tirelessly to get approval to develop Clare Creek Mountain Park. He first ran on a platform of saving the park. And his net worth has increased a great deal in the time he's been in office."

"How dare you accuse my husband – of what?"

"Your family's original home was on the mountain, wasn't it? Your great-grandfather gave it to the city. How can you not work to keep the park from being developed?"

"You're an interloper, not a native. You know nothing of local affairs."

"Please, everyone knows your husband is best pals with the CEO of Black Development. What kind of payback does he expect when the mountain development is approved?"

"If you spread such talk around you can expect to hear from my husband's attorneys, Ms. Locke. And by the way, have the police checked you out in regard to your husband's death?"

I crossed my arms and favored her with a sour grin. "Oh, I could have and would have liked to stomp him into the ground. Nearly did. But my legs aren't that long."

She glared at me. "What the hell do you mean?"

"I was in Georgia, actually in the company of a cop, when my non-beloved ex was murdered." I smiled sweetly.

"Have they checked on your whereabouts? He was at your home. Before you pushed your husband down the stairs and he kicked you out, of course."

Suddenly her skillfully applied makeup was stark on her pale face. But she crossed to the sofa table and looked down, said nothing.

I wasn't going to get anything out of her, obviously. Why had she gone back to her husband? And why was he not allowing her near him? Abusers generally wanted their victims nearby. But maybe she had finally had enough, pushed him down the stairs and he didn't want to take a chance on further retaliation. Somehow that didn't seem likely to me.

I turned toward the door and reached for the handle. I heard quick footsteps behind me and started to turn around. Something hard crashed into my head. The lights went out.

Thirty-One

My head hurt. I was being dragged across something rough. With each bounce the pain exploded through my head. My mind couldn't grasp what was happening. Where was I? What happened? Flashes of thought came between bouts of sharper pain. Rhoda Jarvis seemed to be involved.

Shock shot through me like an electric current. I'd been in her hotel room. The bitch had hit me, knocked me out. The pain in my head receded from my full attention. I tried to reach up to my head but I couldn't. My arms were confined somehow close to my body. And now I realized I could hardly breathe. I must be wrapped in a rug or something else thick and fuzzy.

Just then the dragging stopped. Through my cocoon I felt something, or someone, lift my legs and lower body. The person - Rhoda? - grunted several times with the effort. Then I was propped up in a slanted position, head down on a hard surface. A chill enveloped my whole body as the certainty of what was happening hit me. She was going to throw me over the dam, too.

Now I didn't seem to be bound so tightly. Maybe the rug or carpet had loosened a fraction from the dragging. I strained to move my arms, legs, any part of my body. No good. A rope or something held it around me. My mind raced. I tried frantically to think of a way to save myself in the few seconds I knew I had. The small trees and bushes growing out over the spillway. If they would snag whatever I was wrapped in maybe I could get one or both arms loose and grab them. Such an impossibly slim chance but all I had time to think of doing.

My upper body was lifted up and then the weight of my legs and lower body pulled me over the top railing. Just as I felt myself start to fall I tried to throw every muscle in my body violently to the left. When I jerked I felt a sudden loosening of whatever was wrapped around me. It began to unroll and pull away. To my great good fortune it unrolled to the left. I was dumped across a tree and the one next to it. I flung my arms around both small trunks and held on for dear life. My weight pulled both trees down at a perilous angle but they held.

My feet scrambled wildly for purchase on the rock strewn side of the spillway. I dared hope one would hold but it slid away and rolled down. It landed with a muffled thud, possibly on the rug or blanket that had been wrapped around me. At last my toes caught a crack and I tried to ease a bit of my weight from my tree saviors.

I tried to make as little noise as possible. Rhoda Jarvis might look over the railing and glimpse me hanging onto the side. She needed to think I was lying dead among the rocks. I tried to muffle my harsh and panicked breathing and push down the fear that threatened to overcome me. I listened. Was that a car starting up? Light flashed across the top of the dam and was gone. Headlights. So she was gone, thank God.

Okay. Think back to the view of this overgrown spillway when Jake and I stood at the overlook. Bushes and trees like the ones I clung to lined and overhung its side from top to bottom. Their profusion was easily seen from the overlook but not from above. The steps of the dam itself were sloped, wider at its top than its base, but the spillway, not stepped, angled down at a steeper angle.

I could try to more or less crab-walk down the concrete side by catching hold from tree to tree. But then what? Below the dam the small amount of water that spilled over the dam from the reservoir flowed through a deep ravine with steep sides. The road ran along the side of the ravine but there was no way I could climb up to it. No good.

So. Try to crab-walk up? My arms and shoulders were already tiring. Even if it were possible, I didn't think it was possible for me. Not now. Only one other alternative presented itself. Crab-walk down, rest a bit at the base where Gloria and Emory had landed, and carefully walk up the probably slick steps of the dam. Attempt to climb over the fence. The fence across the dam which was higher than the one at the top of the spillway.

I made up my mind to start down just as the thin clouds that had obscured the quarter moon moved from its face. Visibility increased enough to help a little. Inch by painful inch, spindly tree to weak, scrubby bush, I made my way down the thirty or forty feet to the bottom of the spillway. My feet dislodged more small boulders and they rolled down ahead of me. I tried to ignore them.

My arms and legs began to shake uncontrollably when I finally arrived at the bottom. Every inch of exposed skin was scratched and bleeding. The outfit I'd worn to dinner was a disaster. What did it matter? I was still alive. I collapsed on a flat rock and put my head on my arms. When I raised my head after several minutes and looked up the stepped face of the dam my mind quailed at the thought of that climb. I couldn't do it. But I had to.

A picture of those tenacious yellow rose bushes floated before my eyes. I could do it. Or die trying. By rights I should be dead anyway. I waited a few more minutes. Then before I lost my nerve completely I rose and walked across the spillway apron to the step of the dam at that level.

Each step of the dam was broad, about two feet wide. Very little moss or algae grew on the spillways since they had not been used in recent memory to relieve pressure on the dam. But as I'd feared a thin layer of the stuff covered much of the surface of the steps. It grew out across them from the edge of the sheet of water running constantly over the dam. The least amount of moss was near the edge of the steps. As they rose, there would be no trees or bushes to break the steep crash to the bottom of the spillway if I slipped and fell. Before I could talk myself out of doing it I started up.

After only a couple of steps my heart nearly stopped when one of my feet slid sickeningly. I had to remove my shoes, the leather soles were apt to be my undoing. I shoved them into the front pockets of my slacks. I'd need them when I got to the top. If I got to the top.

In sock feet I again began my slow ascent, trying to remember to breathe. After what seemed hours, but was probably closer to forty minutes, I reached the wide top of the dam. I sat down on the barely twelve inch extension of concrete on my side of the eight foot fence. I wrapped my arms around one of the metal bars and dragged in deep breaths for a few minutes. Finally my body's violent shaking eased a little.

Now that I had reached the top I realized that my only option was to scale this fence. To reach the lower fence at the top of the spillway was too risky. I would have to swing out over the spillway and down to the fence. Not tonight. Or not this morning, the time had to be near three or four o'clock. I sat and breathed some more and then put my shoes back on over my filthy socks and tackled the fence. Compared to my crab-walk down the side of the spillway and slick mossy climb up the dam the fence was a piece of cake. At last I stumbled off the dam and fell on my back in the dew damp grass leading to the parking lot.

When I realized my shivering now was from cold as well as pure exhaustion I dragged myself upright and started toward the nearest building, which was the Nature Center. I heard a car's engine as it came up the drive from the direction of the gate. I was next to a large rhododendron bush loaded with large buds, ready to burst into bloom, and dodged behind it. I waited until the car came into view. As it got closer to my position I saw the logo, Storm Security. Of course, I'd forgotten. They made a couple of passes through the park every night. I stepped out from my hidden position and waved both arms. The driver hit the brakes and came to a sliding stop. He cut the engine and jumped out, gun in hand. I kept my own hands in the air.

"Please, call the police and ask for Sergeant Lane. Tell him you're calling for Cameron Locke. He knows me."

He walked toward me slowly, gun lowered slightly. "Ma'am, it looks like you need an ambulance. I'll call 911."

"No. Ok, but first please call Sergeant Lane." "You'd better sit down." He holstered his gun. "I have a blanket in my car. You're freezing."

My teeth were chattering, I realized. I let him lead me to the car and wrap a blanket around me. It felt like heaven. I listened as he called the police station and asked for Shac. He was apparently transferred to Shac. He gave his name and who he was with and told him I'd asked him to call, then handed the phone to me. "He wants to talk to you."

"Shac, I'm in Clare Creek Park. She tried to kill me."

"She? Never mind now. Are you all right? Where in the park?"

"The Nature Center parking lot. Don't ask Dispatch to send EMS or ambulance. Will you come?"

"I'm not far away. Be there in ten minutes. Let me talk to the Storm Security guy again." I handed the guy his phone and leaned back against the car seat. God, I was so tired.

Thirty-Two

Suddenly we heard the roar of at least two big engines coming as fast as they dared up the mountain. Shac to the rescue. Only I'd already rescued myself, I thought. Like I'd rescued myself from Emory Locke. A few hours ago I would have given odds against my making it off the mountain alive. Faint feelings of pride rippled through my exhaustion. But would Shac or anybody else, read Captain Tawson, believe that it had been Rhoda Jarvis who knocked me out, drove me up here, dragged me over to the dam spillway and pushed me over? Not likely and I had no proof. No doubt she would point the finger at the MMM, claim it was them who'd attacked both of us. At least she'd sure be shocked that I'd survived. Would she try again? Why? I'd only asked her why her husband wasn't allowing her anywhere near him. And was he involved in the murders. What could she possibly think I knew that caused her to try to kill me? Did I know something that linked her to the murders of the two women and Emory? Wait. Was Emory at the Jarvis estate to see Rhoda? Not Senator Jarvis?

My thoughts were interrupted by Shac shaking my arm gently. "Cam? My God, you're bleeding. You need medical attention."

Tom, the Storm Security agent said,"She insisted that I not call 911. Just you."

"She's like that. Hardheaded." Shac said. "I'll take her to the ER. I'll have to make a report anyway."

"Me, too." Tom had his notebook out. "Ms. Locke, why were you in the park at this hour?"

"For the record, I was brought up here against my will. You can see I have no car here. You can get the rest from Sergeant Lane later."

I could see Tom wasn't happy about not getting full information for his report, but I was too exhausted to care. Shac thanked him and helped me to his cruiser. He said he'd be back in a minute, walked over and told his backup she could leave. She didn't look at me as she circled around us to leave the parking lot, but I glimpsed her face in profile. She was the undercover officer I'd seen at the MMM meeting.

Shac got in the driver's side and we left the lot also. "The ER for you again, Cam. If you're going to keep getting in these scrapes, you'd better get some insurance."

"Right. I didn't 'get' into this. Someone did it to me." I rubbed my head, feigning more pain than I felt, which would make it a lot.

"How? Who?"

"Who was that officer?" I asked, in as casual a voice as I could manage. "I appreciate you both getting up here as fast as you did."

"Corporal Morrisson. I'll pass it on to her. Now answer the question."

"You probably won't believe me. Rhoda Jarvis pushed me over the fence above the spillway after she'd knocked me out."

"The hell you say. She brought you up here and pushed you over? Why aren't you dead, like the others?"

That was a good question. Why wasn't I dead? Maybe she hadn't hit me as hard as the others. I'd taken her by surprise so she had to act quickly, whereas she'd meant to kill the others and smashed their heads accordingly.

When we reached the hospital the same young sandy haired doctor was on duty who had treated me Saturday night. He tsk tsk'd when he saw the condition of my arms, neck and face. "I wasn't aware that Wexler Bend was a habitat for tigers. Sure hope he's had his shots."

"Ha. Ha. You should be on tv, you're wasted in the ER." Maybe he'd refuse to treat me and I could go home, make like a bear, crawl into bed and hibernate for a year.

"So I'm told. But Mom insisted on a doctor in the family." He dabbed some liquid on the deepest scratches and I nearly came off the gurney.

"Ah, but what do they do when they're off camera? I bet they stick pins in voodoo dolls." He took a wad of gauze and gently spread an ointment over all the scratches and abrasions. The effect of that ministration was as soothing as the first had been excruciating. When I sighed, he said, "See, I can do compassion."

Strong white teeth showed in a wide grin. "I'll leave the bandage off this original trauma, it's healing nicely, though how it has with your lifestyle I have no idea."

Shac pulled the curtain aside and walked in without invitation. "She gonna live, doc?"

"Probably. This time anyway." He rose from his stool, stripping off his protective gloves. He towered over Shac, I hadn't noticed his height the first time he treated me. He looked down at me. "Overnight observation?"

"No."

"Thought not. Though I wouldn't be surprised if I see you again." He sketched a salute to both of us and left.

"Ready?" Shac asked.

I walked out under my own power, but I have to admit it took all I had. The sun was almost fully up. I'd had another stressful all nighter, to put it mildly.

Thirty-Three

Shac led me to his car and I collapsed in the passenger seat. He went around and got in behind the wheel.

He looked at me. "Your car is at the Clare View Hotel?"

"Yes."

"And you went there because?"

"I just wanted to ask Mrs. Jarvis why she went back into an abusive relationship."

"And?"

"And now I'm wondering if Emory went to the Jarvis home to see her instead of her husband." I remembered too late that I hadn't yet told Shac about seeing Emory when I drove to the Jarvis estate.

"What the -? If he … You told me, and Captain Tawson, you hadn't seen or heard from Emory Locke. Why?"

"I didn't lie. I hadn't at that time. It was later that day. And then I went to Georgia right after."

"And you just forgot to mention it when you got back?"

I flared back. "How the hell was I supposed to know he'd be killed before I got back to Wexler Bend?"

He gripped the steering wheel until his knuckles turned white. Took a deep breath. "You went to the Jarvis home, after I warned you not to do it? And what? Saw Emory Locke there?"

"If you'll allow me to answer. I did drive to the Jarvis home. As I turned into the entrance off Wexler Drive Emory was leaving."

"You talked to him?"

"We both stopped, out of shock, I think. He was full of the same old bullshit. He claimed to think I was following him to find out his business. He'd had to keep me in line when we were married."

"Anything else?"

"His parting words were strange. Something about some people having long memories and revenge."

"A threat?"

"Maybe. But now he's the one who's dead. Why?"

"And you don't know if he'd actually been inside the gates?"

"No. Yes. The gates opened and he drove out as I turned into the driveway."

"Were you? Inside the gates?"

"No. Maid, or whoever answered, wouldn't open the gates for me."

"Did you ask Mrs. Jarvis about him?"

"I did. After she asked if I'd been checked out about his death."

"What did she say?"

"Her face went pale and she turned away. Next thing I knew something hard hit my head. Again."

"And you came around while you were being dragged across the ground."

"Sort of. I wasn't really sure what was happening until I felt her drag my legs up on the fence. Then I was terrified."

He looked at me. Anger and anguish played across his face. "You nearly died up there."

"Tell me about it."

"You didn't actually see her face, while you were dragged or when you were pushed over the fence? Right?"

My expression must have showed my hurt and dismay. He hastily added, "I'm not doubting your story. I'm looking at it like a defense attorney would. She could have an accomplice who actually hit you and took you to the mountain."

I said, "Only the most likely one is already dead."

"As far as we know. OK. Let's go get your car."

When we got to the Conference Center Hotel I directed him around the neatly manicured grass and bright sunlit flower beds separating the sections of parking area to the one where I'd parked my car. Only it wasn't there.

"You're sure this is the place?" Shac asked. "Yes, I'm sure." He waited for me to catch up. My ordeal had apparently slowed my thought processing ability.

"She had access to my keys." I realized I didn't even have my totebag. I looked at him. "She must have taken me up there in my own car. So where is it?"

Thirty-Four

Just then another car pulled up beside us. The driver, the same officer who'd backed up Shac when he came to get me on the mountain, got out and climbed into the back seat of Shac's car. Seeing her close up I knew for sure that she was also the undercover officer I'd seen at the MMM meeting. But now she was dressed in a tailored blouse and jacket over creased slacks.

"Cam, meet Taylor Glass. She's with the TBI. Been working with us on a case."

She stuck out her hand and I shook it. "Undercover. I presume? Since Shac just told me an hour ago you were a Corporal Morrisson."

She nodded. "I saw you. Didn't know who you were, of course."

"Right. Just another disaffected citizen, I guess you figured."

A shrug. "I wasn't especially interested in what the citizens were involved in, just there to pick up any information I could."

"About?"

She looked a question at Shac. "I haven't told her anything about the criminal case. We just talked about the murders. And the attempt on her life."

"Murder isn't a crime?" I couldn't resist asking. Neither paid any attention.

Agent Glass said, "Her car is in the park. Way up in the upper parking lot, wiped clean."

We exchanged glances. I voiced the question we all had in mind. "So how did she, or whoever, get down from the mountain?"

"And Candy Cohrn's VW is in a parking garage downtown." Glass continued, ignoring my last question also. I was beginning to feel invisible.

"The car Emory was driving." I said. "So did his killer take him up and decide to send him down the hard way?" My voice trailed off at the end as something occurred to me.

"What?" Shac barked.

A Wexler Bend Police department cruiser pulled up behind Taylor's car. Jake Hunter got out on the passenger side as Don Mears waved through the driver's side window and pulled away. Jake walked over and climbed in the back seat with Taylor Glass. They greeted each other as though they'd already met so Shac must have introduced them at the station.

"Was at the station. Heard about the party and decided to join you. Mind?" He glanced at Shac.

He and Taylor shook heads. "What do you know about last night?" Shac asked.

"That Cam had a narrow escape." He studied the scrapes and scratches on my face. "Looks painful."

"I'll live. Thankfully."

Shac quickly gave him more highlights. "Her car is on the mountain, wiped clean. So how did the person who nearly killed her up there get back down? Candy's car is in a parking garage downtown. Cam saw Emory driving it on Monday." I saw an expression I recognized cross his face as he said that. Shac wondered if I'd told Jake about seeing Emory and not him.

He continued, "So did Emory drive his killer up to the park and the killer drove his car back down? If so, and the killer left it at the parking garage, why wasn't it found before now?"

I must have made some sound. Before either of the others could say anything, Shac looked at me and asked, "What had you thought of just as Jake arrived?"

"I don't think the VW was at the parking garage all this time."

"OK. Where was it?"

"Still on the mountain. I've told you about the old home site, which I think must have been the site of the original Shell homestead. Rhoda's great grandparents' home. It's only a short distance off the paved trail. And nearby is a tall overhanging rock, with vines and all kinds of vegetation forming a sort of curtain in front of it in spring and summer. She could have hidden the VW there."

Taylor was frowning. "What about tire tracks? Wouldn't they be a giveaway?"

I saw understanding dawn on Jake's face. Shac's, too, after a second.

"Son of a bitch." Shac said softly.

Taylor said, "Okay, what am I missing?"

"Not if the ground was already torn up by emergency vehicles." Jake said just as quietly.

She got it, then. "Mrs. Jarvis was left chained to a tree in the park. Was it in the same area as the home site?"

Shac said, "Oh, yes. And if that's the case, Emory's murder was premeditated. Maybe even Gloria's."

"And Candy's was pre-emptive clean up." I said.

Shac sighed. "Now all we need is to find the evidence."

Jake looked at me. "Right now I think one of us needs to find her bed. Why didn't the hospital insist on keeping you overnight - er, day - for observation?"

Shac grunted. "Like they could. I'll drop her off at her place and go talk to the Senator, whether he's up for it or not."

"Jake and I will go back to the station and see if anything showed up in or on the VW." Taylor said.

Thirty-Five

When we got to Wexler Pointe Shac did his routine of checking my place out before letting me go in. An envelope with the Wexler Pointe logo was on the living room floor. Someone had evidently slid it under the door. Whatever it was I did not want to deal with it now. I threw it on my desk. When Shac left I set the alarm, yanked my torn and dirty clothes off and threw them in the trash. I pulled on my polka dot pajamas and fell into bed.

When my doorbell jarred me awake I felt as though I'd been asleep only a few minutes but the clock showed two p.m. Still too early. If Shac was ringing that bell again this soon I was not responsible for what I might say. But it wasn't Shac standing on my porch, looking worried. It was Daniel Traynor. Surprise kept me still for a few seconds and then I opened the door and invited him in. To my utter surprise Daniel put his arms around me and hugged me tight.

He let me go and smiled a little when he saw my expression. "Dammit, Cam. I'm so glad you're all right. Except a little worse for wear, huh?"

I knew my hair was probably all on end and I was standing here in my ratty pajamas, but I didn't care. I sensed that everything was all right between Daniel and me now, even though I didn't know why it was.

"How did you find out I was – a little worse for wear?"

"My contact at the station just told me 'that PI dame fell off the dam last night.'"

"Your old contact moved out of state. Who is it now?"

"A confidential source is – confidential."

I let it go. But decided I'd make it my business in future to find out who his source was. "Coffee?"

"Sure. Point me to the right cabinet and I'll make it."

I pointed, he put coffee in the Bunn filter and turned it on. I excused myself to gingerly pat my face with a washcloth and throw on jeans and a shirt. When I returned to the kitchen he sat at the counter and had two mugs of coffee ready. I flashed back to Shac sitting there when he told me about the two young women who had been murdered and the yellow roses. At least I didn't think Daniel was bringing news of yet another murder. I did hope he could shed more light on the three we had, which included Emory Locke.

"I assume you know now about the relationship of your ex to one of the young women murder victims?" He stated bluntly.

I almost spit out the mouth full of coffee I'd just taken. "The police have released that information?"

"Not yet. They didn't have to. I knew it."

"You knew it? And you didn't tell me when I was at your place?"

"I couldn't."

"Why not?"

"My client told me in confidence."

"Your client? Jarvis? He knew? How?"

"Slow down. Yes. He thought it was tragic that Emory followed in his father's footsteps without even knowing it. As a wife abuser."

"Typical. So remorseful." Then the connection in my brain that had teased me for days finally showed itself. I sank down on the other stool. "Daisy Montague was their mother. I saw an old tabloid picture of Daisy and Jarvis. When Shac showed me Gloria's picture just a few minutes later my subconscious picked up on the resemblance. But it left me."

"Yes."

"When he was involved with Daisy he wasn't married to Rhoda. Did he abandon Daisy and the babies because he needed Rhoda's wealth and social connections?" I couldn't keep the revulsion from my voice.

"You've heard how politically ambitious he was. But his ambitions outstripped his abilities. Without party backing, he lacked the money and connections to go anywhere. Party leaders gave him the ultimatum of giving up his hell-bent-for-pleasure lifestyle and marrying a woman with connections or they'd find someone else. And he caved."

"Did Rhoda know that was the reason he married her?"

"She had her reasons for marrying him."

"Oh. And did he know at the time Daisy had given one of the twins up for adoption at birth?"

"No. He married Rhoda and they traveled Europe for several months for their honeymoon. On her dime, of course. When they returned Daisy got word to him that she had his son, didn't mention the girl, and that she needed support money or she'd go public."

"And then she was killed in the mass shooting."

"He couldn't find out who she'd left their son with. Exactly when he was born nor where she'd had the baby even. He always figured she had given a fake name to the hospital, or wherever she'd given birth."

I hazarded a guess. "So whoever she left him with just dumped him into the system."

"She had a good friend, but she disappeared. He searched for her, too, and found she didn't have a kid. So he gave up."

I drank coffee and thought about that long ago tragedy. I'd been a couple of years older than Gloria and Emory, living in a two parent home, but my father was present in name only. He never held me on his lap or told me stories. Still I missed him when he died. I had always harbored the hope that if I was good enough he'd love me someday. The perfect setup for becoming an abused wife.

The twins hadn't had even that much of a father. At least Emory hadn't. Did Gloria? "Did he ever find out about Gloria's adoption?"

"He never knew he had a daughter. Couldn't find his son. Rhoda didn't want kids. So every year he did something so out of character you probably won't believe it."

"And what was it?"

"Every year on Mother's Day he sent yellow rose corsages to all the new mothers on the maternity floor at the local hospital."

I sipped coffee and eyed Daniel, not hiding my skepticism. "And the press never picked up on that? Put it on the front page?"

"He sent them anonymously. Though one tabloid stringer found out, ran a short story. Jarvis had the paper kill it. Rhoda was out of the country."

"Why yellow roses?"

"Because it was Daisy's favorite flower." Daniel hesitated a second, as if not sure he should finish the story. "They walked on Clare Creek Mountain the one time he brought Daisy to Wexler Bend. They came across your patch of rose bushes bursting with yellow blossoms and she fell in love with them."

"Did Jarvis tell you all this himself?"

"He told me most of it." He paused. "Gloria told me her part."

Now I nearly fell off the stool. "Say what?"

He grimaced. "Uh huh. Shac's going to read me the riot act. Not to mention I could lose my license."

After two weeks in her rented Wexler Pointe condo Gloria began to feel hemmed in. She'd always been active, not one to sit around. But she didn't want to look for an office job here. She'd have to give references. She'd picked up a local newspaper, the Chronicle, while getting groceries and after reading it dropped it in the wastebasket.

She fished it out of the trash and flipped to the want ads. Mostly for fast food workers. Servers at the local steakhouse. Part-time help at the Garden Center for the planting season. That would get her outside at least. She jotted down the address and went to change into jeans and long sleeved shirt.

Just as she reached the address she realized that the rented Mazda might be a little ostentatious for someone applying for a part-time job. She drove past it and on to the car rental agency, exchanging it for a modest Honda Civic. Returning to the garden center she went inside and ask for the manager. The cashier called an employee to take her back to the manager's office.

"Someone to see you, Charles."

He left her at the door and the manager called, "Come in."

She walked inside. The chunky, bald-headed man, about middle age, looked up and did a classic double-take. He seemed to have trouble speaking but finally said. "Can I help you?"

"I'm Gloria. I was going to ask for the job I saw in your newspaper ad. But now I'd like to know why you were so startled when you saw me."

"Sorry, we've filled all the positions we had open." He said automatically, but he kept staring. Finally he seemed to shake himself mentally and went on. "Do you have family here in Wexler Bend, Miss?" Real curiosity was in his eyes as he asked the question.

"Ms.," she said. "And I'm not sure. Why do you ask?"

"Oh, a few years ago we had a guy worked here sometimes. Looked enough like you to be a twin almost."

Her heart immediately sped up, she felt as though it might leap into her throat. She knew the blood had drained from her face. Her brother. Could it have been her brother? She sank into the nearest chair without being asked.

"Hey, you okay? I didn't mean to upset you." He started to rise but she waved him back, said she was all right.

"To tell the truth, I came to town looking for a possible family member. What was this man's name?"

"Emory Locke. About your age, I'd guess. We teased him because he resembled the owner of the business. He didn't take it too well."

"The owner? Who is that?"

"If you're from out of town you probably wouldn't know him. He's the State Senator from this district, Senator Wiley Jarvis."

She managed a shaky smile, tried not to show additional shock. What were the odds? The man she'd come to Tennessee to meet owned this business. "No, I don't know him. Maybe this Emory didn't like politicians."

"Most definitely. He left town a couple of years ago after he and his wife divorced."

"Bummer. I'd have liked to meet him."

"Too bad." He seemed to hesitate for a second.

She caught it and asked, "Was there something else about this man?"

He still hesitated a little longer, then spoke. "Probably shouldn't say anything, but there was talk. And he wasn't the most reliable person ever worked here either."

"What are you not saying?"

"The talk was he beat his wife. Heard the police were called to their house several times during the five or so years they were together here."

"Sad." She replied. "Is the wife still here?"

"Yeah. Funny thing is, she was head of security at a plant on the other side of town. Go figure."

"Thanks so much for your time. Bye." She had been rude, she knew, but she had to get out. She walked toward the door as fast as she could without actually running.

She stayed close to home for another two weeks. Did some internet searches for Emory Locke. Back issues of the

Chronicle had published the police blotter logging calls to the Locke residence here at Wexler Pointe condos, though they didn't list the unit number. She sat back in her chair.

Somebody else had made a reference to police calls to the complex. Who? She couldn't remember. Wait. The Wesale real estate agent who'd handled her lease of the condo had mentioned domestic disturbances involving a private investigator who still lived in the complex.

She also added to her folder of information about Wiley Jarvis from the back issues of the newspaper. She had a hard time thinking of him as her – their – father.

She'd thought she would confront the man soon after she arrived. But at first he was in Nashville as the legislature was in session. Though strangely, according to letters to the editor and some local news outlets, he was never seen on the floor of the chamber. And after the legislative session ended he took off for Hawaii or else China, depending on the source telling the story.

Maybe a professional could get more information for her. She scrawled a note asking PI Cameron Locke to call her about a possible job and included her phone number. She'd leave it with the leasing office, they could get it to the detective.

One day she happened to be arriving home at the same time as the owner of the neighboring condo. He seemed nice, clean-shaven head, single silver earring, probably mid-forties. They exchanged names, his was Travis Wireman. She asked about the bag he was carrying with the logo of a shop on Main Street that sold expensive imported coffees. She accepted when he invited her inside to sample coffee from the specially roasted beans. The coffee was good and they found a lot to talk about, as he'd lived in Atlanta for ten years. From there he said he moved One day she happened to be arriving home at the same time as the owner of the neighboring condo. He seemed nice, clean-shaven head, single silver earring, probably mid-forties. They exchanged names, his was Travis Wireman. She asked about the bag he was carrying with the logo of a shop on Main Street that sold expensive imported coffees. She accepted when he invited her inside to sample coffee from the specially roasted beans. The coffee was good and they found a lot to talk about, as he'd lived in Atlanta for ten years. From there he said he moved Until one night when Rhoda Jarvis came into the bar area of the lounge with a group of people. They sat at a table and ordered drinks. One of the group had ordered a specialty drink and Gloria had to go to the storeroom for an ingredient. When she brought it to the table Rhoda snapped, "It's about time." But when she looked at Gloria's name tag, 'Daisy,' printed on a large outline of a white daisy, she almost choked and her face went pale.

"Are you all right, Ma'am?" Gloria asked.

The man who'd ordered the drink said, "Good Lord, Rhoda, I wasn't in that much of a hurry. Thanks, Daisy."

"Fine, fine. I apologize." Rhoda said.

Gloria walked away. So that was her father's wife. The one he'd married for her social standing instead of her mother and give his children his name. Next day when she came on duty Travis handed her an envelope. Inside was a letter from Rhoda Jarvis saying they needed to talk. She asked Gloria to meet her when she got off work at a small café on the highway west of town. The letter went on to say that Rhoda knew it was late but she had to wait until her husband was asleep to leave the house.

Thirty-Six

"How – What – Was Gloria a client, too?" *I hardly knew where to start asking Daniel questions. He'd known parts of the story from both Jarvis and Gloria? And never told me, not to mention the police? Shac would sure have him for lunch. And probably Taylor and the TBI would, too.*

"She wrote me from Georgia. Wanted to know how much it would cost to hire me to dig up some information for her. I wrote back, giving my rate per hour, average fees for different jobs. She sent a check. Then she called, told me what information she needed."

"Which was?"

"Anything I could find that wasn't public knowledge about Senator Wiley Jarvis. My red flags went up. One, Jarvis had already hired me to find his son. Two, was there also a daughter out there somewhere?"

"Little did you know!"

"Right. What I did know was enough of a can of worms. I told her I was sorry, but due to the number of cases I was working, I'd not be able to work for her."

"And how did she take that?"

"Tried to talk me into taking her on as a client anyway. I politely but firmly kept refusing. Finally told her I'd return her check and more or less hung up on her."

"But you said she told you – "

He held up a finger. "I did put her check in the mail, it was a box number, and the envelope came back marked 'return to sender.' When I did some digging I found it was one of those drop box mail stations. Further reinforced my decision not to take the case. So I forgot about it. Figured she had just put a stop on the check."

I voiced a guess. "But she moved to Wexler Bend and contacted you in person?"

"In the meantime I was running down any leads Jarvis gave me and sifted through what seemed like thousands of news stories and other records tracing his activities when he partied around the country. Just because Daisy, who claimed to be the mother of his son, contacted him from Georgia didn't necessarily mean that the kid was born there."

"But they were."

"And about the time I discovered that Jarvis had fathered twins, not just a son, and the mother had been killed within a year, Gloria got in touch with me again. Said she had to find her father."

"Wild, isn't it? They were born at New Hope."

"Wild, to say the least."

"The director of New Hope told Jake Hunter a private investigator questioned her several months ago. You?" He nodded. "But she told him it was a Georgia PI."

"I'm licensed in Georgia and Tennessee."

"So you were in a real dilemma."

He stared into his cup. "Oh, yeah. Originally she hadn't said anything about suspecting Jarvis was her father. Just for information about him."

"Go on."

"I told Gloria I still couldn't take her case. She was a little testy. Offered more money. I still refused." He stared into his empty coffee mug. "Suppose I hadn't?"

"You couldn't, Daniel. You told me often enough not to beat up on myself about what couldn't be changed."

He nodded, made circles on the counter with the mug. "I didn't have much trouble verifying that Gloria was the female twin. Her adoption was pretty straight forward. Emory was a different story. If I never have to try to follow a trail through those damn Georgia DHS foster care records it'll be too soon." He looked into my eyes. "But the scariest part was when I finally did get to the end of it."

So Daniel had found the proof of what I now suspected was the reason Emory moved us to Tennessee. "When you found out that my recently deceased husband was his son." It wasn't a question.

He nodded. "I'm not sure Emory really believed he was Jarvis' son. He'd bounced around the foster system so much, he knew nothing about his origins. A guy he knew in Georgia had told him he really looked like a Tennessee politician. He spent a lot of time at the library when you got here, didn't he?"

"He did. I was just glad when he wasn't home. I could relax a tiny bit."

"His library record shows that he studied everything he could find about Jarvis. He insisted you go to work at the garden center, didn't he?"

"Yes. You think he did because Jarvis owned it?"

"No doubt. He finally managed to see Jarvis and present himself as his son."

"Did Jarvis believe him?"

"I hadn't had a chance to give him my findings. It was about the time he found out he had terminal cancer. He put Emory off, told him he'd talk to him after he went through the first round of radiation. Jarvis went to a Texas cancer clinic, just recently returned, still undergoing chemo. You kicked Emory out, humiliated him. Emory left town and returned with a girlfriend he picked up in Florida, Candy Cohrn. Maybe because she was originally from Wexler Bend. He went back to mining the library while she worked at the hotel restaurant."

I refilled both our mugs, lost in thought, trying to piece everything together. The players in this series of tragedies had finally assembled in one place.

"Emory must have thought, a mistake that cost his life, that Candy inheriting the flower shop was a Godsend. Gave him a way to come back under the radar." Daniel said.

Something he had said earlier popped back. "You said you thought Emory didn't really believe he was Jarvis' son. So he came here to run a scam on Jarvis?"

"Yes. But I got a sample of DNA from both, unknown to Emory." Daniel shook his head. "It verified that Emory was, in fact, the Senator's son."

"And what of Gloria? Did you tell Jarvis about her and that Emory really was his son?"

"I told him, of course, when he returned to Wexler Bend. He was happy to hear about Gloria. About Emory, not so much."

Thinking about my ex, I said, "With the Jarvis legacy, he was lucky that one turned out well."

"He's not doing well himself. Gloria's death before he could get to know her hit him hard."

I suddenly realized that Daniel didn't know about Rhoda Jarvis. Or that she was now the prime suspect in all the murders because she'd botched her attempt to kill me. But her motive was still something of a mystery. Unless Daniel's story provided it. He must have picked up my thought vibrations.

"Cam. I'm sorry. I haven't asked much about what happened to you. What were you doing up at the dam? And how the hell did you fall? And the sixty-four dollar question, how did you survive?"

I swallowed too much coffee and strangled, giving me a few seconds to think of something to say. "It's a long story. Hadn't we better get down to the station so you can tell your story before Shac comes after you?"

Daniel narrowed his eyes. He was a damn good private detective and could smell a delaying tactic a mile away. "You don't want to tell me. Or can't?"

"Truthfully, I don't want to go through it again by talking about it. And I can't either. But I will tell you about it. After you talk to Shac."

He rose from the kitchen stool. "What the hell. Might as well face the music. Can I work for you after I lose my license?"

"Don't be so negative. That's what you told me. There were extenuating circumstances for you. Plus you've got a friend in high places."

"For how long? Shit. That was a sorry thing to say."

"Forget it." I grabbed my car keys and the spare tote bag I'd pulled out of a closet to replace the one Rhoda Jarvis probably threw in the reservoir. "Damn. My car's in impound. You'll have to drive. Just a minute. I'd better make sure they're there." I picked up the phone and dialed Shac's direct number.

"They?" Dan asked. "Who's working with him?"

I hadn't mentioned Taylor Glass and the TBI to him yet. I held up a finger as Shac's phone began ringing and stopped almost immediately as he answered.

"Why aren't you still asleep, Cam?"

"Daniel and I are coming in to talk to you. Are you free?"

"Why? You or him got some new information?"

"Ummm. Yeah. He needs to tell you something."

He didn't say anything for a few seconds. "Get in here then."

I noticed the envelope from the Wexler Pointe office and stuffed it in my tote bag. "Let's go."

Thirty-Seven

We didn't talk much on the way in. I really didn't know what would happen to Daniel. Except I was certain it would not be pleasant. Shac did not like for information to be withheld. Couldn't blame him. He'd have to explain it to Captain Tawson.

Shac was waiting for us and led us through the door leading to the Detectives' squad room. We passed his desk, picking up Jake and Taylor on the way. The parade continued as we entered the short hallway with three doors leading to two interrogation rooms and the observation room between them.

Shac opened the first one and motioned for Taylor and me to enter. We did and Taylor closed the door. "Get you some coffee, Cam?" She asked.

"No. What I'd like is an explanation. Why am I in an interrogation room?"

"This is Sergeant Lane's plan. I'm just here to make sure you're comfortable."

She looked just as fresh and creased as she had the last time I saw her, early this morning. Even her makeup looked freshly applied. While I still felt like I had bed head and was grungy since I'd not had time to shower.

"Suppose I decide to just leave? I've done my civic duty." I felt like a traitor for what I said next, but I was fishing for information. "I brought Daniel in for questioning after —"

"I was told to keep you here by whatever means necessary." She smiled. "After what?"

"Nothing. Never mind." I decided to push my luck. "Is this the way the TBI treats attempted murder victims?" "Am I mistreating you, Cam? I offered coffee. Would you rather have tea, a soft drink, something from the vending machines?"

"God, no. I've had stuff from the vending machines here."

She smiled again. "If I was an envious woman, I'd envy you. Escaped from a murderer, not enough sleep today and probably not enough food, scratches all over your face and you still look good."

I stared at her. "Bullshit. That window is mirrored on this side. If you need a reminder of how you look."

A couple of seconds later the hall door opened and Shac entered. He nodded to Taylor and she went out. He took her chair. "What was that, a mutual admiration society between you two?"

"A person uses whatever she can to find out what's going on."

"Aren't you angry with your buddy, Daniel, for holding out on you? Or is that why you brought him in?"

He knew me too well. "So why am I in an interrogation room?"

"Protocol. Just run over the story he told you and you're outta here."

I didn't say anything. I was aggravated because I knew what he said was true. But I was still pissed. And tired. And not enough sleep, as Taylor had said.

"Start when he got to your place, time, et cetera. You know the drill."

Sighing loudly, I started talking. Told him about Daniel waking me up and prefacing his story with the statement that he'd probably lose his PI license. Shac nodded. When I finished I said, "My turn. What does Senator Jarvis say about all this? Did you tell him about his wife trying to kill me?"

"Doesn't work that way. You know I can't talk about the case with you. You're free to go. You'd better get some more rest. You still look bushed, with good reason."

"Can Daniel go, too?"

He just looked at me and got up to open the door. He motioned me through it and led the way back to the squad room. When we reached his desk I sat down in the visitor chair.

"He could be here a long time."

"Okay. Got any magazines or boring old reports I could read?"

Shac turned and went back toward the interrogation rooms. I felt a little sorry for Daniel. But it was tempered by being pissed that he'd known Emory was in town and hadn't told me. Exactly what good it would have done me to know, I wasn't sure. Except I would have been even more afraid that it was him throwing rocks through my bedroom window. And who had, if not him? I couldn't quite picture Rhoda disconnecting electric lines and hurling rocks. On the other hand she did seem to have an obsession with rocks.

Thirty-Eight

After half an hour in the chair I was getting antsy, as Shac knew I would. I was pretty sure he hoped I'd get antsy enough to leave. I studied the row of pictures of 'persons of interest' taped on the wall behind his desk.

When I tired of looking at bearded, bleary-eyed persons the police wanted to talk to for a variety of reasons, I started digging in my tote bag. The envelope from the condo complex office that had been shoved under my door. My notebook. Extra toothbrush and other stuff I wasn't going to pull out here in the squad room. No wallet. Or drivers license. Or PI license. I could lay the hassle of getting them replaced squarely on Rhoda Jarvis. Damn her.

Nothing I wanted to read so I ripped open the condo office letter. Two pages. The one on top was a letter from the office apologizing that the enclosed message for me had been inadvertently put in a file instead of being delivered to me. When I looked at the other note I could hardly believe what I read.

'Ms. Locke, I need your help in locating someone with whom I need to talk. My own efforts have been futile and another person I asked has been less than helpful. Please contact me at your earliest convenience at the number below.' It was signed, 'Gloria Tejoso.' The date at the top of the note was eight months ago. The note wadded up as my hand did an involuntary spasm.

Before I could digest the meaning of the note the door to the squad room opened and the desk sergeant on duty looked at a pretty olive skinned woman and gestured toward me.

The woman, about my age, looked nervous as she walked across the room. I got up, offered her my chair and moved to Shac's desk chair. "Are you looking for Sergeant Lane?"

"Yes." She looked relieved. "The officer at the desk said a Sergeant Lane was handling my cousin, Gloria's – case" Tears filled dark eyes fringed with naturally long lashes and she reached into her thick tapestry purse for a tissue.

"Oh. You're part of her adopted family. I'm very sorry." I didn't remember if either Jake or Shac had mentioned that Gloria had family. Of course, it was likely. I just hadn't considered it. "She didn't have any children?"

"No, and she and Peter divorced. Mama was sad about it, was glad Grandmama was not alive to know about it. But I wasn't. Gloria needed her, they could have talked."

I got the idea the cousin meant more than talking about the divorce. She hadn't given her name so I gave her mine, hoping she'd reciprocate. "I'm Cameron Locke."

"My name is Juanita Tejoso. My father is Carlos Tejoso, now the only child left of Grandmama's. We haven't heard from Tia Luisa since Tia Teresa died when Gloria was a baby. They were beautiful, models."

Beauty ran in the family, apparently. Juanita could have been a model herself. So could Gloria. But she'd been a bartender.

"Your family always lived in or near Atlanta?"

"Yes. But my husband and I want to buy a mini farm in a development called Canna Lily Farms, north of the metro area."

My face must have shown surprise and so did hers at my reaction. "Would it be near Fallon?"

"You know it?"

"Lived there a couple of years, when I was a kid." I backpedaled in a hurry. Didn't want to visit those memories again. "Long time ago. You were close to Gloria, growing up?"

"Oh, yes. But not so much when we grew up. She studied and went to college. Worked in an office before and after she married Peter. I married and stayed home to raise our son and daughter."

"I see. Have you kept in touch with her after she moved to Tennessee?"

"A little. I was happy she found love again here. I thought maybe she'd give up looking for her biological father."

"That's why she came here?"

"She was obsessed with finding him after I gave her the picture of her real mother. She was shot at a fancy party in a hotel."

"How did a picture of her mother bring her to Wexler Bend?"

"When Grandmama died Gloria found more things, papers, another picture of her mother and two babies, not just one, and a newspaper clipping. If she had only stayed in Atlanta she would still be alive."

Maybe, I thought. Her mother had died in Atlanta. I glanced at the note crumpled in my hand. A fleeting thought I didn't want to entertain whispered that if I'd gotten the note earlier, Gloria might still be alive.

Just then Shac, Jake, Taylor and Daniel all came bursting through the hall doorway. Shac was shouting into his phone. "Make sure that corridor is secure. Find her. Now."

He slowed long enough to look at Juanita, apparently realized who she was and motioned for Taylor to take care of her. He grabbed my arm and pulled me along with him as Jake held the door of the squad room open. Daniel trailed behind.

"Cam, go home. You, too, Traynor. We'll get back to you."

"Oh, no, Sergeant Lane." Daniel insisted. "He's still my client. I'm going to the hospital."

"No, you're not."

"What in God's name has happened?" Shac still gripped my arm, but I had to shout to make myself heard over their argument.

"The Senator's wife tried to get to him," Daniel answered. "And I am going. You'll have to arrest me to stop me."

Shac snapped,"That can be arranged."

"Is he hurt? Is Security holding her?" I yanked my arm from Shac's grip.

Jake was already in Shac's car. Shac shoved me toward Daniel. "You two stay together. Do not get in the way. Do I make myself clear?"

We nodded and hurried to Daniel's car. He didn't waste any time, but he wasn't able to keep up with Shac, running with siren wide open and flashing blue lights clearing the way. "Well, is she in somebody's custody or not?" I demanded.

"Apparently not, from what I heard. Hospital security and his own guy were on the corridor, saw her trying to sneak into his room. Stopped her, but she got away." Daniel kept his eyes on the road.

"The woman must be Houdini." I said. "Three murders and no witnesses until now."

"She was a would-be actress, you know. Tried to go the Hollywood route and all. Until her father dragged her back and made her marry Jarvis."

"A marriage made in heaven." I said. "Or smoky back rooms."

"That was Gloria's cousin back at headquarters, wasn't it?"

"Yes, pretty broken up. Blames herself some that Gloria came to Wexler Bend." I wondered if Daniel felt any self-blame because he could not work for Gloria. He'd been in a difficult position, true. But two women, and my unlamented ex, were now dead. I wouldn't have wanted to be in his place. I shoved the thoughts aside.

"Hold on." Daniel took a corner nearly too fast but kept control. We came into sight of the hospital. The grounds and parking lot were a sea of blue lights. It was obvious we weren't going to get anywhere near the place. Daniel pulled over the curb and onto the grass a block away and killed the engine.

Gloria drove out of town on Old Town Road. It narrowed when she passed the city limits sign and she slowed her speed, searching for the sign for the Stop In Cafe. Finally by the light of a dim street light a hundred yards away she saw the faded sign. "What the – " There was a closed sign in the dirty front window. A tattered 'Business for Sale' banner hung across the top front of the low building, one end hanging loose. She pulled in to turn around and look at the note. Surely she'd read the name wrong.

First, just in case, she pulled on around to the back of the building. The area between the building and the steep slope behind it was just wide enough for one car. Then she spotted the front of a big car backed into what must have been the service entrance of the café when it was open. She drove closer to the car and tried to see if anyone was inside but the dim light and darkened windows made it impossible.

When Mrs. Jarvis, or anyone else, didn't emerge from the car after several minutes, Gloria opened her own door. The thought that it might be a risky thing to do occurred to her briefly. But no one was around. Maybe the woman had taken ill and needed help. She walked around the front of the black Lexus. A faint shuffling noise sounded behind her and she half-turned just as something slammed into the back of her head. She fell to the ground unconscious.

She didn't feel herself being dragged around the big black car. Her assailant, dressed entirely in black and wearing gloves, dragged her into the yawning trunk and slammed it closed. The person then entered the Lexus and pulled it out and away from the service entrance, got out and left it idling. The driver then got in Gloria's Honda, engine also idling, pulled it forward and backed it into the place where the Lexus had been hidden. When the person, dark as a shadow, was again behind the wheel of the Lexus, the car crept forward and, after a few seconds, drove through the small parking lot and away.

Dampness on her face brought Gloria partially back to consciousness. She couldn't understand what was happening. Her thoughts swirled in confusion. Then she realized she was being pulled through dew dampened grass.

But where was she? The grass ended and she was dropped on a hard surface, like concrete. Somebody rolled her over roughly.

"Awake, are you, Daisy? Good." Above her a low voice spoke, harsh with hate and anger.

"Who? Mrs. Jarvis? What..."

"I expected one of you would turn up some day. I took care of your whore mother, but couldn't find you or your bastard brother. None of you will get a penny of my money."

"You had her killed? Where's my brother? Is he dead, too?"

"Soon. Too bad his wife didn't finish him off. Would have saved me the trouble."

Filled with anguish that she would now never know her brother or her father Gloria tried to rise. But the woman picked up one of the large rocks nearby and ended that torment forever.

Thirty-Nine

We got out and started walking toward the mass confusion. As we passed a pair of spreading magnolia trees I felt someone grab my arm and almost jerk it from the socket. Since both arms were still very sore from my climb down the dam spillway I screamed. Daniel turned around at my scream just as I felt a circle of cold metal under my chin. "Get back here, Traynor, or I'll shoot you both for interfering in my affairs."

If possible I was even more terrified than I'd been just before she dumped me over the spillway fence. I knew I'd never even hear the bullet that ripped through my lower jaw, palate and the frontal lobe of my brain. I tried to stand very still, so as not to provoke her.

"You don't want to fire a gun this close to all those police. They're tuned to gunfire." Daniel ambled back toward us, talking softly.

"Maybe. But at least this thorn in my side will be dead. Keep walking to your car. We'll be right behind you."

"I have to hand it to you, Mrs. Jarvis. Hard to see how you got out of the hospital without being seen." Daniel was still using a soft, soothing voice. Evidently trying to flatter the bitch to bring down the tension I felt vibrating through the arm that held me and the gun under my chin. I doubted it would work. She had gone over the edge.

I guessed Shac and Captain Tawson hadn't expected her to go after her husband with his own and hospital security around him. But I still didn't know her actual motive for killing Gloria and Emory, her husband's biological offspring. Had she somehow found out that he was their father? I didn't know, and if I was going to die at her hands this time, I wanted to know.

We'd reached Daniel's car. Her voice was steely as she ordered him, "Open the back door very carefully, then get behind the wheel. Remember I really want this woman dead. If I'm caught at least I'll have that satisfaction." She'd have to move the gun from my throat when we got in the car. Maybe I could use her irrational hatred to get her off guard. She did move the gun from my throat only to shove it sharply into my ribs, still very painful from my night on the mountain. I couldn't help grunting loudly. She laughed. "Remind you of your loving husband, dear? He thought he was a big man, just because he knew how to disconnect an electric line and throw a rock. He learned better after I took care of his sister."

I grunted again. "You did know."

"Drive, Traynor. And don't pull any tricks. A bullet in the side will kill her just as well as one to the brain. What did you think, Ms. Locke? That I killed them for the fun of it?"

Before I could answer she gave Daniel more directions. "Cut across Industrial Drive to the By-Pass. I'll tell you where to turn off." Daniel did as she ordered. She added,"And don't speed."

"You wanted to know why I went back to my abusive husband. My lawyer told me that with all his powerful friends, he'd get most of the money if we divorced. Even though it was my money and connections that got him where he is. And I was his punching bag, too, all those years. I couldn't let everybody know how he humiliated me. That would have come out, too, in a divorce action." She jammed the gun harder in my side. "Newspapers love a high profile divorce."

I couldn't help it. My anger rose and I baited her. "But I managed to throw off my abusive husband without having to go through a court trial. You couldn't stand that, could you?"

"Cam." Daniel said warningly.

"Let her taunt me. My revenge will be sweeter when she's begging for mercy." Rhoda gave a high, demented laugh. I tried to repress the shiver that went through me, but she felt it and that demented laugh came again.

Then her words echoed through my mind. Emory had said something similar. "You told him you were going to kill me."

He loved it, the fool. He had no idea I planned all along to kill him first. He and his sister had to go. Just like their mother."

"Huh?" I blurted. "You were behind the shooting massacre that killed Daisy?"

"I met all kinds of people in Hollywood. But I took sick, pneumonia, and Daddy called it a nervous breakdown. Made me come home and marry a cheap, dumb politician. The promoters of that party at the Majestic made snuff films. Overseas. I paid them to shoot one in this country. Who knows how many times people have seen her for what she was. She thought she could extort my money from Wiley. Just because he fathered her kid. Even he didn't know she'd had twins. Neither he or I could find either one, though he didn't have any idea I was looking."

The woman was wicked, evil. I could hardly bear to be so close to her. It was hard to credit, but she made her husband look almost saintly by comparison.

"He thought I was in France. But I saw that news article about him sending yellow roses to new mothers every Mothers Day. And all the time knocking me around, choking me. He hated me. He wanted babies and I couldn't have them because of a botched abortion in my teens."

She shouted to Dan, "Exit here and turn right."

I glimpsed the creek and realized she was taking us to the Jarvis estate. I tried to slow my breathing and think. If the gate was closed, she'd have to open it. How? Did she have a remote control on her somewhere? If not, someone would have to let us in. But if there was any live-in help, they would have been instructed not to allow her inside. So, she must know there wasn't anyone there. To activate a remote control she would have to loosen her iron grip on me. I had to hope she had one and waited to seize any opportunity to overpower her. She was strong, had height and about thirty pounds on me. But I was strong, too, and had training and desperation on my side.

Forty

When we reached the entrance driveway to the Jarvis estate, Rhoda shouted again, "Turn."

Dan braked and turned into the driveway, continuing up to the area in front of the ornate gates. He asked, "How do we get in? Do you have a remote?"

I felt her reach with her left hand and open the car door. Since she was left-handed she was holding the gun just a little bit awkwardly against my side with her right hand. I knew this would be the only chance I had. I flung myself flat on the seat and kicked, trying to push her out of the car. I screamed Daniel's name as the gun discharged. The explosion so near my ear deafened me and I felt the bullet whiz by only an inch or so above me.

Even with all the simultaneous sensory input I felt the car jerk forward. Daniel had stomped the accelerator when I screamed. Since it was a straight drive, even with the transmission in park it jerked enough to throw Rhoda off balance. She fell out of the car door, though she held on to the gun and it fired again. That bullet took an upward angle and barely missed Daniel on its way through the roof of his car.

I grabbed the door handle on the other side and scrambled out. When I rounded the back of the car I saw Rhoda and Daniel on the ground. He'd managed to open his door and get out, too. He'd tackled her to the ground before she could make it to her feet after falling when I kicked her out. He was grappling with her for the gun.

"Console. Gun." Daniel managed to gasp out. The woman was strong for someone who'd never done a day's work in her life. Daniel was not a big man and they were about the same weight and height.

I leapt through the driver's side door and ripped open the console between the seats. I grabbed the pistol lying on top of the jumble in it. Just as I turned with it in my hand I heard Rhoda's gun explode again. In horror I saw her push Daniel off, his blood gushing out over the print scrubs she wore.

"Bitch. You shot him," I screamed. And emptied the clip into her body though she managed to get off another shot that grazed my head on the right side.

I threw myself down beside Daniel, balled up the front of his shirt and pressed both hands into his wound. I knew it was futile, but I couldn't let that thought in. "Oh, God, Daniel. Don't die. You can't die. Stay with me. Help will be here in a minute."

My mind scrambled for something to grab through the fear for Daniel's life. I didn't know how I'd call for help with no phones. Wait, maybe the bitch had hers on her. But I couldn't stop pressing, had to stop the bleeding. My mind raced, trying to find a solution.

Daniel's eyes were closed, but suddenly they opened. Fear flared in them. "Where is she?" His voice was barely audible.

"I shot her. Stay with me, Daniel."

"Afraid not, honey." He paused, trying to breathe. "Envelope in my desk. For you. Thanks for going to the prom with me, Cam." His eyelids fluttered closed again and he exhaled a last soft breath.

"No. No." I moaned and kept pressing on his wound even though I knew it was useless, unaware that tears streamed down my face and mixed with the blood pouring from the gunshot to my own head.

Suddenly red and blue lights and sirens converged on the driveway, lighting up the manicured lawns and flower beds. I didn't know how they'd been summoned, but it didn't matter now. Daniel Traynor, my friend since childhood, was gone. He'd died saving my life. And I could never thank him for it.

Forty-One

An hour later I was in a room on the second floor, just down the hall from the one in which I'd found Louise Shackleford Taggert whispering over a sleeping Shac. I shoved the memory aside. Then the vision of Daniel, lying on the ground, his life bleeding away under my frantic efforts to stop it. Finally alone, I let the tears silently flow for my friend.

"Cam?" A soft voice spoke my name. "Is it okay if I come in?"

I wiped my eyes with the corner of the sheet and croaked. "Come in, Zoey."

Her eyes looked too big for her small face as she parted the curtain and came to stand beside my bed. She tentatively touched my hand and her eyes went to the bandage that was threatening to become a permanent part of my attire. "How are you?"

"I'll live, so the doc says. You heard?"

"It's all over the news. Cam, I'm so sorry. I should have trusted you."

I waved her words away with the arm the IV was attached to and grimaced as it pinched. "Why? I had no real reason to go after her at the time. And she was a pillar of the community, as they say. You would have been risking your job."

Another knock on the door sounded and Tabi's voice spoke my name. "Cam, may we come in?"

I raised my eyebrows at Zoey. "Sure, Tabi, come on in."

But when she came in Tabi was pushing a wheel chair. Zoey stepped back to give them room beside my bed. An extremely thin man sat in the chair, an oxygen tube trailing from his nose to a tank on the back of it. It was hard to reconcile the wasted man in front of me with the handsome robust young politician with a beautiful blonde party girl on his arm.

"Senator Jarvis." I said, and stopped. What do you say to the man whose wife you killed earlier in the evening?

"I understand I owe you, Ms. Locke. Rhoda would have kept coming for me, I'm sure, until this cancer put me beyond her reach permanently."

"Well." I didn't know how to answer that.

"And I am sorry for my part in fathering a son who abused you for years. If I had provided a real father figure for him, he may have turned out differently."

"Maybe. But Emory had choices. We all do." I didn't mean it to sound accusatory, but he nodded in acknowledgment of the statement.

Jarvis sighed. His hands fluttered in his blanket covered lap. "My greatest sorrow is that I didn't get to meet the daughter I never knew I had. Now there's no one left, of Rhoda's family or mine."

Yet another knock sounded on my door. Until this case I never realized I was so popular. "Come in," I called.

Juanita Tejoso peeked around the curtain. "Oh, you have company. I'll come back."

"No, come in, Juanita. There's someone you should meet."

She came on through, eying the man in the wheel chair. Since she was far from stupid I figured she guessed his identity.

I tried to sit up a little straighter and Zoey helped me. "Senator Jarvis, this is Juanita Tejoso, your daughter's cousin in her adopted family. Juanita, as you know, the Senator is Gloria's biological father."

I saw a brighter spark come into the Senator's eyes. "Juanita. I'm very happy to meet you."

Juanita took his hand gently in hers. "And I, too, am happy to meet you."

Jarvis's voice was noticeably weaker when he said to her, "I think I must rest a little now. But will you come to see me later? I want to hear all about my daughter and the family who loved her."

"Yes, sir. I will." She watched as Tabi wheeled him out, waving to me and mouthing that she'd see me later.

I belatedly introduced Zoey and Juanita, who hit it off immediately. After a few minutes of get acquainted chatter Zoey noticed my eyelids drooping, hard as I tried to stay awake. "Let's go to the coffee shop, Juanita, and let Cam get some rest." They left, promising to see me later or in the morning.

Forty-Three

I was released from the hospital the next morning, with strict instructions to go home and rest. Shac and Taylor were waiting in front to pick me up when I was wheeled downstairs. "Jake gone back to Georgia?" I asked. I felt a twinge of disappointment that he hadn't stopped by to say goodbye.

"Told me to tell you he's going to work to get that hotel shooting cold case opened up again." Shac answered.

Taylor said, "And you're dropping me off at the airport to fly back to Nashville. My bosses say Black has dropped plans for the mountain park development, so it's moot."

"That's good." I said. "I wish Gloria could know."

We didn't talk much on the short drive to the airport. Shac and I watched from the car as her puddle jumper commuter plane took off and then he started the engine.

"Don't take me home just yet."

"You're going home, doctor's orders."

"I have to go by Daniel's office. It's important."

He hesitated. "What's important?"

"Just before he died he said there was an envelope in his desk for me. I need to see what he was talking about."

"You're sure you're up to it?"

I nodded. Not really sure but I had to go.

We reached Daniel's subdivision and I had to swallow hard when we turned into his driveway on the side of the neatly tended yard. I dug out the key he gave me when I worked for him and he'd never asked me to return. We entered his office, which had a separate entrance from the front door. I paused on the threshold to get a grip.

"We can do this later. Whatever it is will still be here, Cam."

"No, he said it was important." I walked over to Daniel's desk and opened the top drawer. As he'd said, an envelope was there. The fat envelope had my name on it.

I dropped into Daniel's desk chair and held the envelope for a minute. Shac stood beside me a moment, then went and sat in a side chair upholstered in gray and white plaid.

I opened the envelope and pulled out a sheaf of papers. One was Daniel's official Tennessee private investigator's license, the second his license from the state of Georgia. The third was a letter that began, 'Dear Cam,' but my eyes filled with tears I had to dash away before I could continue reading.

'I'm heading to your place in a few minutes. After I talk to you I'll go to the police and tell Shac everything I know about the victims in the recent murders in Wexler Bend. I'll probably lose my PI license after I do that. You'll see why after I've told you everything. I'll probably leave Wexler Bend, if I'm not in jail, and find something else to do.

So I'm signing my house and business over to you. You'll just have to register the business with the Secretary of State in your name. The transfer documents are signed and notarized through my attorney so you shouldn't have a problem. I have no family left, as you know, so I've also named you as beneficiary in my will. Hopefully that won't come into play for a few years, but I'm just saying.'

The letter also was notarized. He apparently hadn't wanted to take any chances on the legality of the documents. The deed to his house, corporate transfer papers, and the letter all swam together through my tears. I threw them toward Shac and put my head down on Daniel's desk blotter, sobbing.

I heard the papers rustling as Shac read them. Then the room was silent for a few minutes except for the sound of the water gurgling in the fish tank with no fish. I felt Shac's hand on my shoulder, as he tried to comfort me.

"He thanked me for going to the prom with him our senior year. His dying words. Who would have imagined nerdy Daniel Traynor would die a hero."

Shac knelt in front of me and took both my hands in his. "He did, indeed." He made me meet his eyes. "And thanks to both of you, Gloria and her mother Daisy Tejoso can both rest in peace now."

Thank you for reading my book.

If you enjoyed it, won't you please take a moment to leave a review at your favorite retailer?

Thanks!

Books by Sylvia Nickels

Requiem for a Party Girl is the first in my Cameron Locke, Private Investigator mystery series, set in East TN.

Cam's second adventure is chronicled in *Delusion for a Lonely Girl*, and her third in *Anguish for a Wasted Girl*

Sylvia's other books published by A Different Drummer Publishing.

A standalone novel set in Georgia will soon be available in print as well as ebook.

Sweetwater Deception

Print and ebook:

Best Served Cold, Revenge a la Carte

Life Slices, A Medley of Musings after Three Score and More, volume of columns

Eight Miles of Muddy Road, memoir

Love Comes Home, romance shorts, writing as Mallory Marrs

Ebooks available online at Amazon and Smashwords, as well as other venues:

Just Deserts, sci fi flash fiction

Sweetwater Deceptions, standalone mystery

Lucky in Alabama, love story

Secrets and Lies, shorts anthology

ABOUT THE AUTHOR

Sylvia Nickels lives and writes in the Appalachian foothills of East Tennessee. Much of her writing is set in that beautiful area. She is a member and webmaster for Lost State Writers Guild, long-time regional writers' group.

Sylvia has published two mystery novel series.
Requiem for a Party Girl, *Delusion for a Lonely Girl* and *Anguish for a Wounded Girl* feature female private investigator Cameron Locke.

The first book in Sylvia's other mystery series, *Disguise for Death*, features Royce Thorne, and was released by The Wild Rose Press.

For a few years Sylvia wrote a weekly column for a local newspaper called *Life Slices*. She gathered some of those columns into a small volume. *Life Slices, A Medley of Musings after Three Score and More,* is available on Amazon and other online venues. Her memoir, *Eight Miles of Muddy Road*, recounts her childhood as a sharecropper's daughter in rural Georgia, and is also available from online venues.

Other books include *Best Served Cold, Revenge a la Carte,* a collection of her short mystery fiction, *Love Comes Home* (under pen name, Mallory Marrs), *Ringer Blues* novelette and *Just Deserts* flash fiction, all available as ebooks.

Connect with Sylvia:
Writing Blog:
http://www.mysterylanerambler.blogspot.com/
Writing website: http:www.ramblinscribe.com

Sylvia's Personal Blog:
http://www.postoakchronicles.blogspot.com
/Personal Website: http://www.sylvianickels.com/

One of the themes in Requiem for a Party Girl is domestic violence and how one woman was able to escape it.

Listed below are the numbers for the National Domestic Violence hotlines, which may be called anytime, 24/7. Also two websites with information to help a person recognize if she (persons of any gender or any relationship can be victims of domestic abuse) is a victim of domestic violence or abuse.

800-799-7233

800-787-3224 TTY

http://www.thehotline.org/is-this-abuse/abuse-defined/

Domestic violence can happen to anyone of any race, age, sexual orientation, religion or gender.

It can happen to couples who are married, living together or who are dating. Domestic violence affects people of all socioeconomic backgrounds and education levels.

If you're beginning to feel as if your partner or a loved one's partner is becoming abusive, there are a few behaviors that you can look out for. Watch out for these red flags and if you're experiencing one or more of them in your relationship, call the hotline to talk about what's going on.

Telling you that you can never do anything right

Showing jealousy of your friends and time spent away

Keeping you or discouraging you from seeing friends or family members

Embarrassing or shaming you with put-downs

Controlling every penny spent in the household

Taking your money or refusing to give you money for expenses

Looking at you or acting in ways that scare you

Controlling who you see, where you go, or what you do

Preventing you from making your own decisions

Telling you that you are a bad parent or threatening to harm or take away your children

Preventing you from working or attending school

Destroying your property or threatening to hurt or kill your pets

Intimidating you with guns, knives or other weapons

Pressuring you to have sex when you don't want to or do things sexually you're not comfortable with

Pressuring you to use drugs or alcohol

http://www.healthyplace.com/abuse/emotional-psychological-abuse/gaslighting-definition-techniques-and-being-gaslighted/

Gaslighting is a form of emotional abuse where the abuser manipulates situations repeatedly to trick the victim into distrusting his or her own memory and perceptions.(con't at website)

Signs of 'gaslighting'

You constantly second-guess yourself.

You ask yourself, "Am I too sensitive?" multiple times a day.

You often feel confused and even crazy.

You're always apologizing to your partner.

You can't understand why, with so many apparently good things in your life, you aren't happier.

You frequently make excuses for your partner's behavior to friends and family.

You find yourself withholding information from friends and family so you don't have to explain or make excuses

You know something is terribly wrong, but you can never quite express what it is, even to yourself.

You start lying to avoid the put downs and reality twists.

You have trouble making simple decisions.

You have the sense that you used to be a very different person – more confident, more fun-loving, more relaxed.

You feel hopeless and joyless.

You feel as though you can't do anything right.

You wonder if you are a "good enough" partner.

www.ingramcontent.com/pod-product-compliance
Lightning Source LLC
Chambersburg PA
CBHW050930120626
46552CB00001B/141